## PRAISE FOR AMERICAN TUMBLEWEEDS

With *American Tumbleweeds*, Marta Elva pulls us into the minds of a half-dozen members of a border family in crisis, dramatizing the state of living *ni aqui, ni alla*—neither here nor there geographically and emotionally. A moving first novel.

— John Sayles, film director, author, and MacArthur fellow

The aptly named *American Tumbleweeds* depicts the balancing act some bi-cultural families must undertake to live in America. The characters indeed "tumble" back and forth over our southernmost border, forced to live in two worlds at once. This is an experience all Americans should know about.

— Sonia Manzano, author of *Becoming Maria:*
*Love and Chaos in the South Bronx*

Marta Elva's debut novel, *American Tumbleweeds*, provides an engaging look at the human cost of the turbulent 1960s along the Mexican-American border. Deftly conveyed through the eyes of an innocent and vulnerable fourteen-year-old girl and her family, this well-written saga could just as easily reflect contemporary times. It is insightful, timely, and rich with meaning.

— Pam Webber, author of *The Wiregrass*

Marta Elva has written a coming-of-age novel that perfectly captures the feel, fear, fun, and uncertainty of the late 1960s. I was hooked on this delightful story from the very first page. And the characters stayed with me long after the final word.

— Melanie Payne, *The News-Press*, Fort Myers, Florida

*American Tumbleweeds* is an engrossing, enlightening portrayal of life along the Mexican-American border in the late 1960s. Marta Elva's sensitive insights draw a straight line to family and societal issues in today's headlines.

— Annamaria Alfieri, author of *Strange Gods*

*American Tumbleweeds* is both a moving coming-of-age story and a compelling tale of border intrigue that goes back in time to give a human face to some of the most divisive and hotly debated issues facing contemporary America. Marta Elva shows an uncanny knack for dialogue and plot as in each chapter she moves back and forth among her characters, unrolling the narrative through each individual's unique point of view.

— Michael Winship, senior writer, *Moyers & Company*, PBS

*American Tumbleweeds* is a story right out of today's headlines, lovingly written by Marta Elva with characters and scenes that reach straight into your heart.

— Robert N. Macomber, award-winning
author of the Honor Series

Marta Elva tells a story so concise and compelling, I felt I'd exchanged identities with each of her characters. Once I started this book, I couldn't stop. Set in the 1960s, complete with historical detail to validate its authenticity, it also emerges as a timely tale, reflecting what happens when lives are touched by the effects of immigration. Its final pages brought me to tears.

— Mary Ann Donahue, TV producer and writer

The setting and time-frame of *American Tumbleweeds* would be enough to make this a fascinating book. But Marta Elva brings every character to vibrant life by allowing them to speak in their own voices, making this story of family, change, love, and survival even more compelling. An intensely moving, memorable debut novel.

— Suzie Gilbert, author of *Flyaway*

# american
# TUMBLEWEEDS

# american
# TUMBLEWEEDS

# Marta Elva

CIRCLING RIVERS
RICHMOND, VIRGINIA

Book cover and inside design by Jean Huets

Quote on Leavenworth: *Leavenworth Train: A Fugitive's Search for Justice in the Vanishing West*, by Joe Jackson. New York: Carroll & Graf Publishers, 2001.

Devil With The Blue Dress
Words and Music by William Stevenson and Frederick Long
Copyright © 1964 Jobete Music Co., Inc. / Copyright Renewed
All Rights Administered by Sony/ATV Music Publishing LLC on behalf of Stone Agate Music
(A Division of Jobete Music Co., Inc.), 424 Church Street, Suite 1200, Nashville, TN 37219
International Copyright Secured All Rights Reserved
Reprinted by Permission of Hal Leonard Corporation

I Heard It Through The Grapevine
Words and Music by Norman J. Whitfield and Barrett Strong
Copyright © 1966 Jobete Music Co., Inc. / Copyright Renewed
All Rights Administered by Sony/ATV Music Publishing LLC on behalf of Stone Agate Music
(A Division of Jobete Music Co., Inc.), 424 Church Street, Suite 1200, Nashville, TN 37219
International Copyright Secured All Rights Reserved
Reprinted by Permission of Hal Leonard Corporation

I Think We're Alone Now
Words and Music by Ritchie Cordell
Copyright © 1967 EMI Longitude Music / Copyright Renewed
All Rights Administered by Sony/ATV Music Publishing LLC,
424 Church Street, Suite 1200, Nashville, TN 37219
International Copyright Secured All Rights Reserved
Reprinted by Permission of Hal Leonard Corporation

Tramp / Written by Lowell Fulsom and Jimmy McCracklin
Copyright © 1986 Budget Music and Universal Music - Careers
All Rights for Budget Music Administered by BMG Rights Management (US) LLC
All Rights Reserved Used by Permission
Reprinted by Permission of Hal Leonard Corporation

# CIRCLING RIVERS

PO Box 8291
Richmond, VA 23226
www.circlingrivers.com
info@circlingrivers.com

ISBN: 978-1-939530-01-1 (paperback)

*for Michael*

# Contents

# american
# TUMBLEWEEDS

# winter 1966–67

# ❙❙❙

## 1   INEZ

**The stranger is in my house, and at home I'm expected to respect my elders.**

THE PURPLE SKY turns blue as I lower the clear red lollipop from my eye. The blue sky stretches over the flatlands spreading like brown sugar across the Chihuahuan Desert. Mountains in the distance surround the huge valley of the United States and Mexico. The Rio Grande flows like a snake between El Paso and Juárez, and the brownish gray peaks of the Franklin Mountains loom close like elephants stomping right through El Paso.

I still miss the old neighborhood where we rode bikes on the streets and roller-skated on sidewalks. This neighborhood is too quiet. People are hardly ever out on the streets, although it's fun living at the foot of the Franklins. Just yesterday, a mountain lion was reported crossing Scenic Drive, the road right above us that cuts through the side of the mountains. I can't wait to see the creature so I can show off to my brothers.

I shove the lollipop in my mouth. The cinnamon candy feels hot against my tongue. Its spiciness warms my body. I take off my coat and continue up the street.

My family moved from El Paso's lower valley to Highland

Park last year. We didn't want to leave but Papá stopped paying the bank for our house and we had to get out. I miss my bedroom with shiny tile floors and a real door.

The house we moved into is old and small. There's only one bedroom with real doors, and we no longer have a shower. I like it, though. The bathtub has feet that look like claws, and there's a little fireplace with a mantel where I hung stockings at Christmas. Mamá doesn't like this house. I can tell because she's never planted a garden.

A black car is parked by the curb in front of my house. All of our relatives drive shiny bright cars with sharp tailfins. This car is plain. When I look inside there aren't any toys or clothing left behind. Nothing hanging from the rearview mirror, no rosary beads or necklaces with funny pictures. This car feels creepy, like kids aren't allowed in it. I don't know who it belongs to because my parents' friends all have kids. I dash to the back of the house.

My feet press down on the worn path of straw-colored grass. A short, sturdy fig tree stands in the middle of the yard, its branches all lit up by the fading rays of sunlight. A row of hollyhocks stands like soldiers against the cool shade of the house next door. The pole of my tetherball set rises from the ground in the corner.

The ball droops from the rope until I smack it hard enough so the tether wraps around the stake. It's no fun playing alone, but my friend Laura wasn't in school today. She and I always walk home together after volleyball practice. We're teammates and classmates, but Laura had stomach cramps. Our seventh-grade teacher, Mrs. Rogers, smiled when Laura's sister Liz dropped off a note from their mother. All the girls know why Laura isn't in class.

At least people don't stare at Laura's body like they gape at my chest. It isn't so bad now that I'm thirteen but when my chest started bulging at twelve—ugh! I still hate the bra.

I whack the ball again. At this time of day only Juana, our housekeeper, is home. Even if my brothers were here they wouldn't play tetherball.

After a few more whacks at the ball, I head toward the house. The kitchen door opens before I reach the stairs. A man with blue eyes peers at me from above.

"What's your name?" the stranger asks.

The black skinny tie hanging from the collar of his white shirt matches his suit. Mamá says *los Americanos* dress up for the strangest occasions. Removing the lollipop from my mouth, I try to speak. No words come out. Who is this *Americano* and why is he in my house?

"What's your name?" he repeats.

"I-nez," I stutter.

"Do you live here, Inez?"

Would I be in the yard if it wasn't my house? I want to ask. "Yes, sir."

"Well, come inside then."

My fingers search for the magic charm hanging from my neck. The neckline of my blouse blocks the small marble swirling with color. The charm is a gift from my grandmother, Abuelita Amalia. I discovered its magic. If I rub the marble, someone always comes to my rescue.

My heart thumps. I return the lollipop to my mouth and twirl it quietly. I'm not supposed to talk to strangers, but the stranger is in my house. At home I'm expected to respect my elders.

"Don't worry. Juana's inside." The man at the door smiles and gestures with his head.

I still take my time climbing the stairs.

The scent of recently cooked flour tortillas welcomes me home. Then I notice the mess. A rolling pin rests on a lump of dough on the kitchen table. Cabinet doors are flung open. Groceries, pots, and pans have been tossed onto the counters and floor.

Juana sits on the bed we share in the room next to the kitchen. She clutches a Bible to her chest. Her eyes are red. She's been crying! I want to run and hug her, but Juana and I have never hugged before. Another man is rummaging through my closet.

He stops to look at me, then continues, pulling out the brown purse where I hide the pack of cigarettes Laura and I use to practice smoking. He looks inside the purse, then throws it next to a pile of my dresses lying by his feet.

Jerk!

The man who opened the door finally introduces himself. "I'm Agent Flannery and that's Agent White. We're with the Federal Bureau of Investigation."

"The FBI?"

"Are you familiar with the FBI, Inez?"

"Yes, sir, I watch *The F.B.I.* on television every Sunday. You always catch the bad guy."

Agent Flannery smiles. "How old are you, Inez?"

"Thirteen."

"Are you related to Ramón Ramirez?"

"Yes, sir, he's my father."

"Tell me a little bit about your dad. Has he taken any trips lately?"

Papá is a world traveler, and I'm proud to tell that to the agent. "Yes, sir. My dad went to Chicago and Mexico."

"Does your father make many long-distance calls?"

I suck on the lollipop. Should I tell the agent Papá has started to use public telephones? The agent's questions confuse me. Is he saying Papá is the bad guy? I take the candy from my mouth. "Yes, sir, my dad makes calls but so does my mother."

"Oh yeah? Who does she call?"

"Her brother. My uncle in New York."

"Where is your mother, Inez?"

My heart flutters. Did I just tattle on my parents?

# III

## 2 RAMÓN

**Around me, people quietly resume their day, mocking the chaos of my new reality.**

THE DIFFERENCE BETWEEN the United States and Mexico is discipline and order. Everything has a place *en el otro lado.* On the other side of the border in El Paso you don't see streets like Avenida Juárez with rows of tourist shops that sell Mexican crafts ranging from tasteful artworks to gaudy trinkets. In El Paso, cantinas don't cater to underage *Americanos* in the evening.

Ciudad Juárez is where *los Americanos* come to release their inhibitions, indulging in vices deemed too impure for their city. The vitality of the United States turns vulgar in Juárez. Perhaps this is the price of having such an illustrious neighbor *al otro lado.*

I first visited America as a teenager in the 1940s. El Paso's history fascinated me, the way it transformed itself from a wild frontier in the 1900s to one of the largest commercial transportation centers with metal-smelting plants and oil refineries. Mexico was my home, but the energy of the United States appealed to my sense of discovery. More than adventure, America offered promise, the opportunity to start over and succeed if that's your desire.

A tap on the gas pedal of my new Shelby Mustang allows me to cruise through the yellow traffic light. The smooth ride makes me smile as I dodge pedestrians and vendor carts on my way north toward El Paso. My wife, Katalina, doesn't share my feelings about the automobile.

"*¡Qué burla, Ramón!* The children can barely fit in the back seat. It's a joke!"

She's right, yet I couldn't resist the car's shiny white exterior, its black leather interior, front bucket seats, and glossy chrome stick shift. The memory of my wife's voice fades as I glance into the rearview mirror.

Where is Miguel? I recommended my friend as driver for this job. A sour taste seeps into my mouth. I roll down the window, spit, and pull up to the curb to wait.

A young boy approaches with a stack of newspapers clutched under one arm. His other hand carries a shoebox filled with packs of American cigarettes. He offers them to me. Poverty is harsh in Juárez. The Mexican peso can't compete with the power of the American dollar.

I wave the paperboy off. The despair on his face makes me call out.

"*¡Muchacho!*" I gesture toward the newspapers.

The boy beams when I give him a quarter and tell him to keep the change.

"*Gracias, señor.*"

Seconds feel like hours until Miguel's box truck appears. We loaded it with two pieces of Mexican handcrafted furniture: a bed and a table. Items without drawers so U.S. Customs isn't tempted to search the furniture. The truck's undercarriage has been altered to accommodate fifty kilos of marijuana. The cargo bed is lined with thick steel to stifle the pungent fragrance of the product.

I roll up the window and step on the gas. The power of the Mustang causes a pack of Pall Malls to fall from the dashboard and land near my feet.

As I approach the tollbooth of the Paso del Norte Bridge, backed up traffic forces me to stop the car. I pick up the pack of cigarettes from the floor, glancing at the newspaper on the seat beside me. Striking a match, I read the headlines: *President Lyndon B. Johnson and Mexican President Gustavo Díaz Ordaz Settle Chamizal Dispute.*

After checking on traffic, I continue reading: *The Chamizal Dispute will be settled in October almost fifty years after it erupted. The tract of land in question is small but of great significance because of the relationship between Mexico and the United States, a love-hate ambivalence of mutual need and recrimination.*

A common trait in most relationships, I think while rolling down the window.

Cool air strokes my face as I drive up to the tollbooth.

*"Buenos días."* I smile at the clerk.

The toll operator ignores my greeting. I roll up the window, shift the car into first gear, take a quick glimpse at the truck through the rearview mirror, and continue.

The Rio Grande runs under the bridge, a shallow narrow outline lacking distinction, merging nations rather than marking a border. As a student at the University of Torreón, I learned El Paso and Ciudad Juárez were destined to become one of the largest international border communities in the world. The prediction is in progress with cross-border manufacturing and inseparable economies. Nonetheless, the

U.S. Customs and Border Patrol checkpoints up ahead offer tangible proof of the social and political divisions between the United States and Mexico.

Something huge hits my windshield, blocking my vision. I flinch, tightening my grip on the steering wheel. It's a large tumbleweed bouncing off my car. A gust of wind hurls two smaller tumbleweeds across the bridge. I take a deep breath and steady my hand on the stick shift.

Miguel speeds up and pulls beside me. We cruise toward the lanes of traffic waiting for the U.S. Customs' scrutiny. The pounding of my heart continues. It wasn't my idea to accompany Miguel on this trip, but once the order was given, I could not refuse. What will I do if Miguel is pulled over for a random vehicle check?

I roll down the window to let in air. The dashboard clock reads three. Today is my wife's birthday, and I promised to take her out to dinner when she leaves work at five o'clock. I can't be late.

The U.S. Customs agent scurries back inside his booth as I pull up. Where is he going? What's going on? I take one last puff before snuffing out the cigarette.

The agent steps outside again. Drops of perspiration line my brow as he unsnaps the holster of his gun and leans toward my window.

"Please state your citizenship," he instructs.

"American."

"I need identification."

The officer watches as I lean toward the glove compartment. Before I reach it, the officer pulls his pistol and aims at me through the car window.

"Don't make a move or I'll shoot!" he hollers. "Now, slowly sit up and place your hands on the steering wheel."

With a side glance, I see Miguel's truck surrounded by men in FBI and ATF jackets, their guns drawn. Two FBI agents walk toward me, guns aimed at my vehicle. The Customs agent greets them.

"The driver and white Mustang match the pictures you distributed earlier today. I verified them."

"Good job," one of the FBI agents comments. The other agent addresses me.

"Leave the keys in the ignition and slowly step out of the vehicle."

With three guns aimed at me, I can't do anything but tighten my grip on the steering wheel.

"He said MOVE!" The Customs agent swings the driver door open.

Moist handprints linger on the steering wheel. I place a leather wing tip on the ground. By the time my other foot leaves the vehicle, the world has taken on a sense of the surreal. Sounds grow muffled and time stands still.

One of the FBI agents slams my body against the car and frisks me. I flinch when his fingers probe my private parts. A passenger in a passing car gapes and points at me through the window.

"Nice car," the agents says, turning me around. "I hope you enjoyed it. Do you speak English?"

"Yes, sir."

"Is your name Ramón Ramirez?" the other agent asks.

"Yes, sir."

"Well, Ramón Ramirez, you are under arrest for trafficking

illegal drugs. You have the right to remain silent…." The agent reads from a small card he holds in his hand.

His words are loud and clear, but I'm not listening. When the agent finishes reading, his partner places a set of handcuffs around my wrists, so my hands rest bound in front of my body.

"We have some agents over there who want to have a little talk with you." He gestures toward a brick building in the distance. My wrists hurt when he tugs at the handcuffs to pull me away from my vehicle.

The Customs agent climbs inside my Mustang and drives off. Around me, people quietly resume their day, mocking the chaos of my new reality.

I'm in a serious predicament, yet part of me is relieved. Life was becoming too unpredictable.

# 3 INEZ

**The candy shatters into tiny pieces; its
zesty cinnamon scorches my tongue.**

LIKE AN EARTHQUAKE, one shock follows another.

"Your dad was arrested," Agent Flannery announces.

"When—why—why was my father arrested?"

"Ask your mother about that, Inez."

The agent who was searching my closet nudges Juana.

"*Vámonos,*" he says, speaking Spanish with an accent.

Juana clutches the Bible to her chest, rises from the bed
and stops in front of me. "*Dios los ampare,*" she says, asking
God to protect my family.

"Why are you arresting Juana?"

"She's not being arrested. Juana doesn't have any documentation. We're deporting her to Mexico."

The agent leads the way into our living room. As we pass
my parent's bedroom, I peek in. The door of their wardrobe
hangs open. Their clothing is scattered on the bed, their
dresser drawers emptied on the floor.

As soon as the agents and Juana leave the house, I unbutton the collar of my blouse and rub the marble charm hanging from my neck. Inspector Lewis Erskine from *The F.B.I.* television series appears.

"Why was my father arrested?" I ask.

"I can't explain," the Inspector says, shaking his head. "Someday you'll understand."

"That's my parents' favorite line," I gripe.

The Inspector vanishes the instant I dash outside. The rear lights of the agents' car flash red before turning the corner. Across the street, my classmate Lalo stands on his lawn. The thick lenses of his bottle eyeglasses shimmer when he turns toward me.

Jerk! Lalo is such a gossip. I bet he can't wait to tattle to our class about what he saw. I ignore him, walk inside, and slam the door behind me.

The silence of the house screams my thoughts loud and clear. Is Lalo the only snitch here? Who told the FBI agents about Papá being a world traveler and that Mamá makes phone calls? Will both my parents be arrested?

I shove the lollipop in my mouth and twirl it around. Without thinking, I chomp down. The candy shatters into tiny pieces. Its zesty cinnamon scorches my tongue and mouth.

# III

## 4 RAMÓN

**I know how much children need their father's guidance.**

THE AGENTS ESCORT me toward the brick building. The temperature has dropped; my every breath freezes in mid-air while perspiration runs down my back. A blast from the heating system greets us when we step through the door of the brick building. My body shivers.

Employees gaze as I'm led down a stuffy corridor with bad lighting. We stop at the entrance to a room. When the agent raps his knuckles against the door, his knock sounds like a warning rather than a request to enter.

"Come in!" a voice yells from inside.

Rays of sunlight pour through the window, overpowering the glow of fluorescent fixtures. The bright room is a sharp contrast to the bleak corridor I was led through.

The two men in the room offer another study in distinction. One agent is dressed in a custom-tailored wool suit. His partner wears the cotton blend of a department store purchase.

My mother taught me to recognize fabrics. She designs and creates fashions. When I was young every member of the family was expected to work in her shop and contribute to her efforts.

At the moment, I can only blame fatigue for my focusing on such trivial details.

"He's all yours, *amigos*," says the agent who walked me from the bridge.

"Thanks, Tom!" says the cotton-blend suit. He stands next to a bookcase by the window. The wool suit is sitting in one of three chairs strategically placed: two chairs facing one chair at a wooden table.

I'm grateful when the wool suit gestures to a seat at the table, rescuing my legs from the disgrace of buckling under me. I start to sit but the handcuffs make it difficult to get a good grasp on the chair.

"Here, let me help you." The cotton-blend suit speaks with a Texas drawl. His cowboy boots and long legs appear to move ahead of his torso as he walks toward the table.

I nod, not trusting my voice to remain steady. As I sit and lean back against the chair, the fabric of my shirt clings to my back with perspiration. Tiny beads of water seep through my hairline.

"Let's take those things off so you can remove your jacket," the wool suit says, passing a key to the cotton blend who unlocks the handcuffs.

I rub my wrists without removing my jacket.

"Look, we don't have all day," cotton blend says. "Now do you want to remove your jacket or not?"

"No, sir, thank you."

"How long have you lived in El Paso, Mr. Ramirez?" The wool suit starts the interrogation.

"Sixteen years."

"And you still haven't lost that accent, *Ray-mon*?" The cotton-blend suit mangles my name. I've grown tired of correcting *los Americanos*.

"Where did you live before?" the wool suit asks.

"Juárez. My wife and I moved there from a small village outside of Torreón, Mexico."

"Your wife was born in the United States, but she lived in Mexico?"

"Yes, sir." It startles me that the wool suit knows this information.

"Is that why you married her, Ray-mon?"

The agent's slurs and the heat of the room turn my tension to anger.

"Did you marry your wife to get a green card?" he insists.

I stop myself from launching at the agent. Katalina's citizenship had nothing to do with our marriage. It wasn't until we arrived in America that we learned her birth in this country could help me with the process of naturalization.

"Mr. Ramirez, you and your friends have been under surveillance for months."

"You and the boys were mighty sloppy, Ray-mon." The cotton-blend suit walks toward the table removing a pack of Winston cigarettes from his pocket. "It can take years to catch the pros. You guys have only been together—what—a year?"

The agent offers me a cigarette. I refuse it.

The wool suit speaks again. "This morning we picked up Roberto Rivera at the Greyhound Bus Terminal attempting to ship a large quantity of marijuana to Chicago. His brother Alejandro can't be found. We can cut a deal if you help us find him."

I say nothing. Silence is my only salvation.

"Look, Ray-mon, you're making this hard on yourself. Roberto won't give up his brother, and Miguel is too low on the totem pole to matter."

It's offensive hearing the cotton-blend suit describe Miguel's arrest so callously.

"Mr. Ramirez, our records show your family profited very little, if any, from your venture. You can benefit from a plea bargain."

The agent in the wool suit not only dresses well, he has manners. His partner, on the other hand, needs lessons in etiquette. J. Edgar Hoover has trained these men well. Playing the good cop and the bad cop comes so naturally.

"When was the last time you were in Mexico, Ray-mon? And did you travel with Miguel or Alejandro?"

"How long have you known Alejandro?" the wool suit asks.

I stir in my chair. The only sound in the room is the buzz of the fluorescent fixtures overhead.

"All right, then, let me ask you this. Do you know that Alejandro has turned in family members to stay out of prison? He's not the kind of person you can count on. "

I try to suppress the jolt running through my body. I've heard about Alejandro's associate being tortured to death and his family threatened with the same fate if anyone testified against him. Supposedly, Alejandro turned in one of his cousins for the murder. By the time I discovered I replaced that associate, I was too involved in the venture.

"May I have a cigarette?" I ask the cotton-blend suit.

He removes one from the pack, takes a lighter from his pocket, snaps it open, and flicks the igniting wheel. I draw hard on the cigarette and slowly exhale. The stagnant air causes the smoke to linger as if it's frozen in space.

"Ray-mon, I bet you haven't even considered your family's welfare. Am I right?" The cotton-blend suit sits and draws the chair close to the table. He smiles at me from the other side. "Men like you seldom do. Let's see. You have three kids, all teenagers. Hmmm…Tough age. Ray-mon, don't you remember how much you needed your father's guidance at that age?"

My fists clench, itching to punch the cotton-blend suit in the face. *¡Pendejo!* The fool has no right discussing my family. Of course I know how much children need their father's guidance. Mine died serving his country.

My father served as a captain in the Mexican Revolution. Four years after the conflict ended, Papá died when the train he was riding derailed somewhere between the states of Coahuila and Durango. My brother Emilio and I were toddlers. When we came of age, his service awarded us an education at the military academy in Torreón, Mexico.

Moisture clings to my shirt. Fortunately, my suit jacket hides the perspiration.

"So can we count on your help, Ray-mon?"

The heat in the room suddenly grows unbearable. I should remove my suit jacket, but that would expose my wet shirt to the agents.

These fools are not going to see me sweat.

# III

## 5   KATALINA

**How come people don't make fun of French or British accents?**

"Crazy...." Country singer Patsy Cline croons about the hazards of love. Her sultry voice clashes with the clamor of industrial sewing machines crammed into the concrete walls of Fisher Slacks Manufacturing, Inc.

I often brood about such things myself. With pride badly bruised, I cry out in anger when my husband, Ramón, flaunts his infidelity. I demand the respect that should be part of any marriage. By the time my tears dry I have surrendered to all the reasons for staying: my children and the hope that things will get better. Truth is, I don't want to give up on my marriage.

Music softens the sharp edge of a cruel reality and makes us feel better. Like most Mexican-Americans at Fisher Slacks, my musical preferences are wistful Mexican ballads or *corridos* and *rancheras*. When it comes to the music of *los Americanos*, I favor Elvis Presley, although Patsy is a good alternative.

Fisher Slacks doesn't provide music for our entertainment. It's played to ease the monotony of our tedious labor.

"I don't know how you do it," Ramón often says. "I'd go *loco* with boredom working in that factory."

"*La fábrica* provides for the children," I snap back.

Ramón is a hard worker with high expectations. Last year he quit a good job at the El Paso Department of Sanitation.

"*No puedo*," he said, "I can't drive a truck all my life. I'm looking at something else." He offered no details.

"Does this *something* come with benefits?"

"You don't understand the need to be challenged."

Ramón is convinced the lack of a formal education affects a person's aspirations. I never attended university like my husband, but that didn't squelch my love of learning. Books are my academy. Literary classics, romance novels, science fiction, and dictionaries—all add to my knowledge and language. Magazines keep me up-to-date on the latest fashions.

Ramón knows this and encourages me. He even urged me to learn English. After attending several classes, I decided my free time was better spent with my children. It didn't help when people laughed at my accent. How come people don't make fun of French or British accents?

Now, I speak English only if it's an emergency. Otherwise I depend on my children for translations. Fortunately Fisher Slacks doesn't care about language skills. Their only concern is your legal status.

It's been fifteen years since I started working at *la fábrica*. I'm grateful for my job and thankful for the electric equipment that allows me to stitch slacks in minutes. It's a far cry from the foot treadle and hand crank of the Singer sewing machine I learned to operate in Mexico.

Ramón's mother, Amalia, is a *modista*. Back then she

owned a successful couture venture—her fancy phrase for a dressmaking shop. We were all expected to help.

"*Pon atención, Katalina,*" Amalia instructed. "The performance of this machine depends on the operator, so pay attention and maintain a steady rhythm on the pedal."

I stood up to the challenge, mastering the noisy equipment. The skill proved useful in getting a job at Fisher Slacks Manufacturing. Every job has shortcomings—like this heavy corduroy fabric. It releases a fine dust that clings to everything, including human nasal passages. Still, stitching slacks beats working from sunrise to sunset in the onion fields of Texas and New Mexico.

The backbreaking work was not the only challenge in the fields. I recall the first time Ramón and I stopped at a roadside café after a long drive through the hot desert. The waitress rushed over as soon as we entered the restaurant. She pointed to a sign: *No Dogs, Niggers, or Mexicans Allowed!*

My throat, already parched by thirst, grew dryer. The hunger pangs in my stomach disappeared. I rushed out of the building. Tears blurred my vision but I quickly wiped them away. I was warned about *discriminación*, but didn't expect to experience such madness so soon after our arrival in America.

Ramón caught up to me. "Katalina, people will always discriminate about something. Even Mexican Indians are disrespected in Mexico. Then you have the bias of religion, money—bigotry is endless. We can't let these *idiotas* stop us from moving ahead. "

"*¡Tontos!*" I screamed toward the building. "It's inhuman to withhold food and water from people."

I hate to admit Ramon was right. When my Spanish great-grandmother, Maria de Jesus, married my great-grandfather, Anselmo, a native of the Kickapoo tribe of Coahuila, their *mestizo* children were shunned by Spanish relatives. I try not to think about such things anymore, but at work my thoughts are my only companions. They entertain or torment.

The shrill of electric clippers helps to clear the clutter in my head. The piercing noise comes from the cutting room where men stoop over long tables, clipping patterns from sheets of fabric. The patterns are rolled into bundles, loaded into carts, and delivered to us seamstresses.

The commotion and my thoughts stop as a loud buzzer signals the end of the workday. The music and clatter of equipment is quickly replaced by the hum of employee chitchat.

After turning off my machine, I stand and toss the last pair of corduroy slacks into my work bin. I run my fingers through my short hair, untie my apron, and remove four gold bangles from my purse.

My income allows me to buy nice toys and clothing for the kids. When Ramón worked for the Department of Sanitation, I even treated myself to a few pieces of fine jewelry and a coat with a faux fur collar. Two of the 14-karat gold bangles are a gift from my husband. Ramón has always been generous, although he can be reckless with money. Lately, his spending has increased. He even invested in a *cantina* in Juárez.

"*¡Feliz cumpleaños!*" someone hollers as I turn to leave my workstation. Jimmy, one of the inspectors, blocks my exit. "I hear it's your birthday."

"Yes, I turn thirty-five." I try to pass him.

Jimmy's a handsome twenty-five-year-old. *Los chismosos*, the gossip mongers, claim he has a crush on me. They're correct but we're both married, and as a married woman I must discourage him. Jimmy extends his arms for a celebratory embrace. I offer my hand. He pouts, studies it, then kisses it gently.

I yank my hand away and look around. Fisher Slacks employees smell scandal and live for romantic indiscretions. I leave Jimmy without saying a word.

With heart pounding, I pass the wall lined with cylinders of fabric. Next to them, metal shelves hold bulky spools of thread in a variety of colors and textures. The little bobbin spools in matching hues are stored in plastic containers. I check the pockets of my dress. *La fábrica* fires people even if they take supplies from the building accidentally.

My friend Lupita is at the end of the line of people waiting by the exit. She's a true Mexican-American, born and bred in the United States. Movie stars are her obsession. She even dyes her hair blonde and styles it like Doris Day's.

"Look at you, *mi'ja*." Lupita's high-pitched voice causes people to turn when she addresses me. "You look like our number one actress Miss Elizabeth Taylor, with your fancy dress."

"*Por favor*, Lupita, don't embarrass me," I whisper.

"*¡Órale!*" The man butting into our conversation is *El Güero*, nicknamed for his blonde hair and light skin. "Hey, man, you think Katalina's sexy now, you should've seen her when she first came to work at Fisher Slacks." El Güero unrolls a pack of cigarettes from the sleeve of his tee-shirt. His arms are vibrantly tattooed from wrist to elbow.

"Pray tell," Lupita encourages him.

"Katalina wore these tight skirts, but it was this little bracelet on her leg that was so-o-o sexy." El Güero's hand twitches as if it's burning.

"*¡Basta!*" My frustration makes everyone giggle.

The security guard rescues me. He checks my purse for stolen merchandise and waves me through the doorway.

Outside, the winter sun is fading. I breathe in the fresh air and search for the white Mustang, hoping to find it idling by the curb. Lupita catches up to me as I'm putting on my leather gloves.

"So where is Ramón taking you for—"

"Did you tell Jimmy it was my birthday?"

"I might have mentioned it."

"*¡Chismosa!* You're a gossip and a rat."

"It's not my fault Jimmy's in *lust* with you. He'd leave his wife if you—"

"And what exactly would I do with him?"

A mischievous smile crosses Lupita's face. "Hmmm. I have a few suggestions."

We giggle like girls.

"You're a troublemaker."

"And you're so serious, *mi'ja*. Ramón should know you've got a young stud crazed with passion. Maybe then he'd pay attention to his wife."

Nobody likes to hear their partner's shortcomings described so bluntly. I'm glad when the Fisher Slacks courtesy bus pulls up.

"See you *mañana*," Lupita says, leaving to board the bus. She hollers back, waving. "*¡Feliz cumpleaños!* Have a wonderful birthday!"

"*¡Gracias!*"

By five-thirty the parking lot is empty and the desolate street grows menacing. Fisher Slacks is located in the Second Ward. The neighborhood, known to residents as *El Segundo*

*Barrio*, is a mix of industrial buildings, modest homes, and tenements. Generations of Mexican-Americans welcome friends and neighbors, but are suspicious of strangers.

I move closer to the entrance of the factory as daylight fades. Perhaps I should go inside and telephone Juana to see if she's heard from Ramón. As I approach the door, Jerry, one of the supervisors, walks out.

"*¿Qué pasa, Kat?*" he asks. "Do you need a ride?"

"No, *gracias*. I'm waiting for my husband."

"Go inside. You shouldn't be out on the street all alone. *Buenas noches.*"

Once indoors, I stand by the window. Jerry looks back from his vehicle. I turn away, embarrassed. As soon as he drives off, I leave the building for the public bus stop.

The heels of my shoes click hard on the pavement in the deepening shadows.

### III

San Jacinto Plaza, located in downtown El Paso, is known as Plaza de los Lagartos or Alligator Plaza. The square once had a beautiful man-made pond that housed alligators. Fort Bliss recruits kept wrestling the reptiles after a night of drinking in Juárez. The creatures were removed and the pond dismantled. San Jacinto Plaza is now just a hub for public transportation.

My mind ticks a thousand questions as I board the last bus toward home. My kids always come into my thoughts whenever I grow tired of Ramón's behavior. My concerns and questions aren't only financial. I worry about disciplining the kids by myself. They act up when Ramón isn't around.

The once-crowded bus is almost empty when someone pulls the cord to signal my stop. A neighbor and I leave the bus together. We say goodbye and I plod home alone.

The brightly glowing television screens peer through windows, like eyes mocking me for being so naïve.

# III

## 6 INEZ

**What the heck is marijuana and was Papá arrested for smoking it with la cucaracha?**

AT HOME, THE oldest brother rules. That's sixteen-year-old Eduardo. Fifteen-year-old Carlitos is next, and I'm the youngest at thirteen. This doesn't stop Carlitos from pestering me or teasing me about my looks, even though people say we look like each other. Some of my friends think my brothers are cute. I don't see it, but girls get giddy around Carlitos and Eduardo. Silly girls.

Today, I couldn't wait for my brothers to get home from school. They found me in the kitchen, sitting in a chair holding tight to my toy monkey, protecting it from whatever was happening around us. My brothers didn't seem too surprised when I told them what had happened. We quietly put back all the stuff the FBI tossed from the kitchen shelves.

"What a mess," Eduardo said, picking up cans from the floor.

"It's the FBI, what do you expect?" Carlitos said with a shrug.

We didn't touch Mamá's and Papá's bedroom. When we

finished straightening up the rest of the house, Eduardo said we could watch TV. We sat on the couch and I was glad my brothers didn't ask too many questions.

Now, I'm worried. Mamá isn't home yet. What will I tell my brothers if our mother was arrested? The theme music of *Gunsmoke* makes me feel better. A few seconds later, Mamá's shadow appears behind the curtain outside the window.

She walks through the door ranting, "How many times must I tell you not to watch TV in the dark?" Mamá takes off her coat. The tone of her voice changes. "*¿Qué paso?*"

How is it parents always know when bad things happen? Eduardo gets up from the couch, turns on a lamp, and shuts off the television.

"Papá has been arrested," he tells our mother.

Mamá gasps and falls into the chair by the door. Her face seems to turn gray. Our mother doesn't cry in front of anyone, so her deep howl frightens me. It feels like hours before she stops sobbing.

Mamá dries her eyes and stands. "Tell me what happened."

Eduardo looks at me. "Tell her, Inez."

My heart races. I'm afraid and excited all at once.

"The FBI was searching my room when I got home from school. They took Juana."

"Why would the police arrest Juana?"

"It was the FBI," I correct Mamá. "And they didn't arrest her. Juana was deported because she had no documentation." I mimic the agent.

"Juana has papers. What else did they say, about your father?"

Mamá's impatient tone makes me nervous. I reach for my marble charm but stop when I see my mother watching.

"They said to tell you Papá was arrested."

"*¿Por qué?*" Mamá insists.

"She didn't ask," Carlitos says.

"I *asked*!" I scream, then turn to our mother. "The man said *you* would tell me."

"You're lying. I can tell," Carlitos says.

"I'm not lying!"

"Yes you are!"

"Stop it, you two," Eduardo scolds.

Mamá insists on a reason why Papá was arrested.

Carlitos answers. "He was arrested for selling that stuff he hid in the tool shed!"

Our mother falls down on the chair again. "*¿Qué dices?*"

Carlitos gives me a dirty look when he sees me staring at him—but what the heck is he talking about? What did Papá hide in the tool shed?

"I once saw Papá and his friend Miguel hide a sack in the shed. When I looked inside, I thought it was oregano." Carlitos shrugs. "Tommy said—"

"Tommy! You told Tommy? Why would you do that? I don't want that boy in this house again, *entienden*?"

My brothers have this thing they do where they talk to each other without speaking. One look between them, and each knows what the other is thinking. I hate it!

"I didn't tell Tommy anything," Carlitos says. "He told me about an article he read that said the Beatles were smoking marijuana and it looks like oregano."

"I don't ever want to hear Beatles music in this house again!"

Carlitos gets my best *now look what you've done* glare. How can we live in a house where Beatles music isn't allowed?

Mamá goes into her bedroom. Eduardo and Carlitos go in the kitchen, leaving me alone.

The verse of a song replaces the questions whirling in my head:

*La cucaracha, la cucaracha / The cockroach, the cockroach,*

*Ya no puede caminar / Can't walk anymore,*

*Porque le falta, porque no tiene / Because it's lacking, because
     it doesn't have,*

*Marihuana pa' fumar. / Marijuana to smoke.*

What the heck is marijuana? Was Papá arrested for smoking it with *la cucaracha*? I rub my marble charm.

For the first time ever, no one comes to my rescue.

# III

## 7 KATALINA

**Las Parcas, los destinos**

AN OLD WOMAN stands with me on top of a mountain.

"I must get back to *mis hijos*, my children," I tell her.

The old woman points a gnarled finger toward the horizon. The landscape is filled with treacherous peaks and valleys.

The recurring nightmare haunted me for weeks. Now, guilt overcomes anxiety. I suspected—no, I knew my family was in danger and did nothing about it.

"*¿Tienes prueba, Katalina?*" Ramón always challenged my suspicions, daring me to show evidence of his illegal activities. Our son Carlitos and the FBI confirmed them today.

I want to apologize to the children but have no words to justify Ramón's behavior, or excuses for my negligence. Last year, the kids suffered the humiliation of being forced out of their home when the bank foreclosed on our house. Now the FBI invades the children's privacy, and their father sits in jail.

Clothing litters the floor with other belongings. From the kitchen comes the clamor of pots and pans as my children feed themselves. *Maldita casa*, this damned house is so small it offers no privacy. My hand trembles over the box of tissues on the nightstand.

Fear prevented me from leaving Ramón. That nightmare is now a reality, a frightening experience I'm left to face alone. My head spins with the new responsibilities in my life: taking care of our family and home until Ramón returns. How am I supposed to do that by myself?

I struggle to sit up in bed and stand, tottering while I blow my nose. Looking around, I make up another list of tasks at hand: pick up my room, feed the kids, get the house back together, call Ramón's mother, and find Ramón.

A dresser drawer is stacked on top of a pile of papers. I lift the drawer. Underneath lies a document torn in half: our marriage license.

*Las parcas, los destinos.* Fate intervenes when we don't have the guts to face our destiny. Am I ready to face the world? No, but it and my children are waiting.

I make sure the kids are fed. After dinner, I take Eduardo aside.

"*Mañana* we must find Ramón. I have no idea where to start."

"We'll call the police station."

My heart breaks when I hear my son sounding like a grown up. I ask Eduardo to help me place a call to Mexico. Amalia needs to know her son's in jail.

The pounding in my heart stops it from breaking. I know what Amalia is going to do: she will blame me for bringing this misfortune on my family.

# III

## 8  RAMÓN

**Who will welcome me home when I'm released from prison?**

SOMETIME AFTER MIDNIGHT a train blows its whistle in the distance. I puff hard on my cigarette. The hall light spills through the small window of my cell door in the El Paso County Jail. I shift my body hoping not to wake the inmate in the bunk bed below.

If I were a religious man I'd be on my knees asking for forgiveness or worse, making promises I couldn't keep. To my mother's chagrin I relinquished my Catholic faith during my college years.

"Marxist literature states that religion is the opiate of the people," I proudly announced.

"¡*Virgen Santa!*" Mamá crossed herself. "Don't bring those Communist ideas into my house, Ramón!"

"¡*Sinvergüenza!*" my grandmother screamed and threw a shoe at me. "I will ask the Lord to forgive such a shameful statement." Amá Lucia dangled rosary beads over my head to ward off evil.

I understood their resentment. After all, I had championed their Catholic faith by participating in religious rituals,

47

even danced with the male troupe Los Matachines during *La Virgen de Guadalupe* festivities.

The disgrace of my arrest is about to surpass the travesty of losing my religion.

I missed dinner at the county jail, but the only thing I crave is a hot shower and a shot of whiskey. The tip of my cigarette burns bright red in the darkness. An inmate snores on a nearby bunk.

Six men occupy this room. Four were playing cards on the cell floor when I arrived this afternoon. The two Negroes and two Hispanics didn't bother to look up from their game.

"Find yourself a bed, Ramirez." The guard gestured to a row of bunk beds.

The scrawny Hispanic kid, who looks like a twelve-year-old, mocked my Spanish accent.

"Tank you?" he laughed when I thanked the guard. "I don't see no fucking tank in here. What are you, a wetback from Juárez?"

"Why do you call your own people wetbacks?" one of the Negroes asked him.

"*Mojados* from Mexico are not my people. Fucking wetbacks make us look bad!"

"Man, you are one fucked up creature."

Everyone laughed except me. Like the agent mangling my name, I'm accustomed to people snickering at my Spanish accent or even confusing it for a lack of intellect. This confusion leads to menial jobs and tedious labor, a frustration difficult to explain to my wife or anyone else.

When I was a student at the University of Torreón, I was encouraged to achieve my highest potential. Now I constantly have to prove myself. It's a challenge I accept for the honor of living in America.

I don't believe in divine intervention. I'm more prone to John F. Kennedy's philosophy: It's not what your country can do for you, but what you can do for your country. It's up to me to determine my destiny. Yet the land of opportunity, like most fraternities in the world, carefully selects the recipients of its rewards. Perhaps JFK would have changed this, but even he paid a price for his aspiration.

The train's whistle seems to have woken two inmates who begin to whisper. I get up to use the toilet in the corner. On the way back to my cot I stop at the small window. Only in America can one find jails with outside windows but then again, we're five flights up from the ground floor.

My finger scrapes against the meshed glass, confirming my captivity. Without clocks, I'm only guessing it's midnight. *Media noche* in downtown El Paso, and bright lights still bounce off the dark sky. The window faces the streets of El Segundo Barrio, where Katalina works. She must've been livid waiting for my arrival.

I wonder how long she waited. Or did she leave immediately when I wasn't there? And what about the kids? Are they frightened by my absence or so accustomed to it that they don't care? The tension builds in my shoulders. I rub the muscles on my back. I should have insisted on calling Katalina but I needed time to think. By now she knows the truth, and her anger at my lateness will seem like nothing in comparison.

I'm used to disappointing women, even though my world revolves around them. Mamá is my biggest critic, Inez my number one admirer. Somewhere in the middle is Katalina. I often wonder if I married her for her perseverance.

It wasn't love that convinced me to make Katalina my wife. I took the opportunity to reconsider my engagement to Amparo when Katalina was banished from her home.

Amparo's family made me feel as if I wasn't quite up to their standards. Even my father's military service and Mamá's thriving business didn't make a difference. It also didn't matter that Amparo and I attended the same university.

From the moment I met Katalina, she looked up to me. Her family didn't have as much influence as mine, and after the night we got in trouble with her father, I couldn't leave her behind. Katalina was just a girl when they tossed her from home.

The circumstances were difficult but Katalina's beauty helped my decision. To this day, she possesses an intoxicating sensuality and natural elegance that makes her stand out in a crowd. Her flawless complexion, dark almond-shaped eyes, and voluptuous lips made her one of the most beautiful women in our village of San Agustin. Even my mother complimented Katalina, saying she was one of the few women who could wear any fashion with style.

Frustration, insecurity, pity, physical attraction—whatever cliché fits, I ended up marrying Katalina.

My question now is: who will welcome me when I'm released from prison: my mother, my daughter, or my wife? Which of these women will not give up on me?

# III

# 9 AMALIA

**Such is the beauty of innocence.**

AROUND EIGHT O'CLOCK last evening, a boy came to our door with a message of an urgent phone call. Emilio rushed to *la tienda*, the neighborhood store with the only phone out here in the outskirts of Juárez. It was Katalina, telling us about Ramón's arrest.

This morning the votive candle my mother Amá Lucia lit for our boy crackles on the bottom of the glass container. It lights up the statue of *La Virgen de Guadalupe* and casts a shadow on the picture of *El Sagrado Corazón* that hangs by the shelf over my bed. Jesus and His Sacred Heart watch me crush a cigarette into the ashtray overflowing with cigarette butts.

I rise from my bed to put out the candle. The liquid wax snuffs the stub before I get there. Dawn's white light seeps through the window. The early morning chill makes me wish our small adobe home was equipped with central heating and indoor plumbing.

After washing my hands and face in the washbasin, I stare into the small mirror while drying off. Lack of sleep is not kind to an aging body. The unblemished complexion I was blessed with is now marked with fine lines around my mouth. They grow deeper with each cigarette.

I reach for my coat and search the pockets for another pack of filterless Faros. I was twenty-one the day my husband died. His physician recommended tobacco to sooth my nerves. Now that I'm fifty plus, it's difficult to imagine that such a filthy habit was once considered therapeutic.

I put on my coat and crouch to add logs to the smoldering embers in the woodstove. A sharp pain pierces my chest before I start crying. I swallow my tears. The rest of the family is sleeping, and I don't want to wake them.

Our house has three rooms, each brightly painted and densely furnished. Emilio, his wife, and their two children sleep in the bedroom on one side of the kitchen. Amá and Sabino's bedroom is on the other side. My bed is located in the corner of the kitchen, the middle room. After buttoning up my coat, I walk out the door to fetch more wood for the fire.

The lights of El Paso sparkle at the base of the Franklin Mountains. Somewhere, *al otro lado*, on the other side of the Rio Grande, Ramón sits in jail. Why would he get involved in transporting contraband? Katalina must have forced him to do something stupid for money!

I didn't work during our marriage. The year Arturo died I returned to my trade. I worked hard to provide a good home for my boys. I enjoyed my work but I was forced to earn a living, unlike Katalina who works to buy toys for the kids and clothes and jewelry for herself.

My mother likes to tell people I was eight when I started making dolls from scraps of fabric and stitching outfits for them. I remember the day Amá accepted a Singer sewing machine for her midwife services. She presented it to me on my twelfth birthday. I was elated, tinkering with the equipment until I learned to operate it, studying pictures to create patterns, adding fancy buttons and trims to make my fashions look professional. I was an accomplished *modista* by my sixteenth birthday.

Life without Arturo would have been glum, if not for two sons and the love of my work. I succeeded in creating a happy home for my family, until Ramón left our village in Mexico. He travelled to *la frontera* with his wife and their two boys.

I convinced Emilio and Amá to leave our village of San Agustin to follow Ramón to Juárez. Soon after our arrival, Ramón moved his wife and children across the border into *Tejas*. I knew Katalina had been born in the United States, but why did she have to take away my family?

"*¡Qué Dios te castigué!*" I cursed Ramón when he announced their departure. "I hope you find nothing but hardship in America!"

My outburst shocked even me. I panicked and sought help from *los curanderos*, healers known to ward off evil. A mother's curse, they warned, is seldom cast off.

"*Maldición de madre, Amalia, es seria.*"

Last night when Emilio returned home with the distressing news about his brother, I knew my curse had cast its spell. I lashed out at Katalina.

"*¡Maldita!* Damn her! And how could Ramón be so weak?"

My anger could not rid me of my guilt. My family watched as I took a bottle of liquor and, even though I never drink, filled a glass to drown my sorrows. My tears and the whiskey gagged me.

"*¡Por favor, señora!*" my daughter-in-law Patricia scolded when I couldn't stop coughing.

I felt silly when Emilio had to rescue me with a glass of water.

*No great mind ever existed without a touch of madness.* Ramón once quoted a man named Aristotle and added another proverb: *The distance between insanity and genius is measured only by success.*

I understand the meaning behind these statements. If a person like fashion designer Coco Chanel displays outrage, her emotional outburst is considered creative passion. My outbursts are considered mean-spirited. No one understands the severe reaction I have to hurt feelings—no one except *mi niña*, my granddaughter Inez. Such is the beauty of innocence.

*Mi niña bella*: Inez is destined to be a beautiful woman. Her beauty originates from the blending of Indian and Spanish bloodlines. Indigenous characteristics: a broad nose, thick lips, and high cheekbones add an exotic quality to her good looks. *Solo una maledicencia*; it's slanderous babble that Inez already exhibits the sensuality passed down from her parents.

I just pray Inez doesn't inherit her father's restless soul. Ramón—*Dios mío*, his independence always challenged my need to keep my family together. Thank God my boy Emilio still needs me and relies on me for everything.

The desert wind dries my tears and blows out the match when I try to light a cigarette. The rising sun splashes the Juárez sky with a kaleidoscope of colors. Our modest hilltop home lacks facilities but offers a *vista de millonario*, a million-dollar view of Juárez and El Paso.

The barren landscape beyond the urban sprawl of Juárez looks beautiful and peaceful in the morning glow. A neighborhood rooster greets the day with a boastful caw. The rhythmic beat of the *molino*, an industrial grinder mashing corn into cornmeal to press fresh *tortillas* for the morning meal, reminds me of San Agustin. But the city lacks the sense of community of my village. I think of Ramón sitting in jail. If only we had stayed away from *la frontera*.

"Amalia!"

I turn toward the house.

"*Te vas a enfermar*," Amá hollers from the door.

Mother is right. I better go in or risk catching a chill.

"*¿Cómo amanecieron?*" I ask once inside.

"We could be better this morning." Amá removes several *jarros* from *el trastero* and places the terra cotta cups on the table.

The scalloped edges of the pinewood hutch are stenciled with bright blue flowers and match the designs on the table. The colorful rustic furniture contrasts nicely with the pale yellow of the kitchen wall. The logs I added to the embers in the wood stove this morning are heating our three-room house. Today, even the heat from the stove can't warm our hearts, and only a miracle could cheer our home.

Sabino sprints from his chair and takes the bundle of wood from my arms. We call him my mother's fiancé, but they'll never get married.

Sabino was born to a Náhuatl tribe in eastern México. They are direct descendants of the Aztec and maintain the Náhuatl customs and language to this day. Sabino barely spoke Spanish the day an officer from the Mexican Army approached him with a piece of paper. He was stunned to discover the X he drew on the paper enlisted him in the military. He served in the Mexican Army, but never again signed documents displaying the seal of the Mexican government. That included a marriage license.

My husband, Arturo, introduced Sabino to our family when Ramón was a toddler. My son and Sabino grew close after Arturo's death. I'm glad. Children need the influence of a father figure in their lives. My own father passed away two weeks before my birth.

I've never noticed the ten-year difference between Amá and Sabino until today. His sixty-year-old body hunkers down in front of the stove with no effort while his weathered hands add wood to the fire. Mother's straight shoulders slump gently, no longer hiding her seventy years of age. She struts slowly toward the stove. Her hand trembles as she pours coffee into the *jarros*. Steam rises from the terra-cotta mugs.

It's hard to imagine Amá was once a *soldadera*, one of the women soldiers who helped the army by cooking food and caring for injured soldiers during the Mexican Revolution. In the Army, my mother served as a nurse, although she often dressed as a man with a cartridge belt across her chest and a rifle over her shoulder when the troops moved us from camp to camp. I was six years old when we started traveling with the military. Only men rode horses. The women walked almost everywhere we went. We carried all the cooking utensils along with newborn children and equipment to set up camps. Amá still speaks of her work with pride and reverence. I only remember being hungry and tired most days.

Sabino throws in a last log. He tries to secure the wrought-iron door of the stove but one of the hinges comes loose.

"*¡Caramba!*" he says, kneeling to fix the door.

"We didn't buy *pan dulce*," I say. In our sorrow we forgot to visit the bakery to buy the sweet bread we have with our morning coffee before the breakfast meal.

Sabino fixes the hinge and closes the door on the stove.

He walks to the kitchen table and sits down in front of a cup of coffee. I sit beside him.

"*Qué pesar esto con Ramón,*" Sabino laments. "It's troubling, this thing with Ramón. But he's a strong boy, he'll be home soon."

Amá starts crying. "What have they done to my boy?"

Emilio walks in from the bedroom.

"Let me get you some *cafecito, mi'jo,*" I say, offering Emilio coffee as he heads toward the washbasin by the wall.

"What's going to happen to Ramón?" Amá asks.

"*No sé,*" Emilio says, sitting down at the kitchen table. "I thought Mamá and I could go visit Katalina to get the details."

"*Buenos días.*" Emilio's wife, Patricia, greets us as she walks into the room. Her thin coat stretches around her pudgy figure as she bends and picks up a tin bucket to fetch water from the tank outside. On the way out she stops and strokes Emilio's head. "So you're staying home from work today?"

Emilio shrugs and pulls away from his wife. Patricia knows better than to question my son's decisions. She smiles sheepishly and leaves the house.

"What time do you want to go?" I ask, breaking the awkward silence that follows.

"Soon," Emilio replies as Patricia returns inside.

She places the bucket of water on the stove to heat up for the children's bath.

"We know Katalina," Patricia says. "Even on the day after Ramón's arrest, she'll go to work and send the kids to school. Why don't we visit her this evening?"

I seldom side with my daughter-in-law against my son, but Patricia has a point.

"God forbid Katalina stays home from work on the darkest day of my life."

Amá Lucia sighs and rolls her eyes at my comment.

"You know I'm right, Amá," I protest. "In my day only widows and spinsters were permitted to work outside the home."

"Women's work is easily ignored at home." Amá sips coffee. "The most humble job can boost a woman's confidence and self-esteem. Earning a living is crucial to a woman's freedom." Amá always sides with Katalina.

"Work should not take a mother away from a child."

"*Recuerda*," Amá tells me, "it was Katalina's work that kept Inez here."

Amá doesn't have to remind me. It was disgraceful how Katalina was in such a hurry to return to work. But perhaps Amá is right. I owe Katalina that favor because from the moment of Inez's birth, I wanted my granddaughter in my home in Juárez, not far away in El Paso. I still recall how the heavens produced a magical sight during the most enchanting event of my life: the day Inez was born.

It was the first time I saw snow falling in the desert. *¡Increíble!* A dusting of snow on the tumbleweeds and *nopales*.

At precisely six a.m., Katalina, who had shrieked in pain through the night, released a soothing sigh as her baby came into the world.

"*¡Una niña!*" I screamed. A girl!

Amá Lucia cut the umbilical cord, secured the stub, then held up her great-granddaughter by the ankles. A swift slap on the rump helped Inez announce her arrival. We wiped her clean and gently placed her on her mother's tummy.

Katalina embraced the small body, touched the baby's

toes and fingers, and promptly fell asleep. I removed my new granddaughter from Katalina's arms. When I wrapped Inez in a blanket, she snuggled against me. At that moment I realized Inez was more than a granddaughter. She was my child, *mi niña.*

After a few days, Katalina insisted on going home. "*Mi trabajo,*" she said.

How could she think about work when she had just been blessed with a child? "What about Inez?" I demanded.

"I've made arrangements for a housekeeper to look after the baby."

"*¿Un extranjero?*"

"I'm not leaving her with a stranger," Katalina argued.

"*¡No es familia!*" Patricia protested. "You have three women here who *are* family."

Amá Lucia made a suggestion, "Perhaps Inez can stay until she's a little older."

Katalina resisted. "Doña Lucia, I came to Juárez because you're the midwife who delivered my other children and I wanted you here for this one. Now we live in El Paso and I want my baby with me."

"*¡Egoísta!*" I accused Katalina of being selfish. "Think of the child."

"I *am* thinking of my baby. I want her with me!"

We debated until I reminded Katalina how she had done everything possible to avoid the pregnancy. My words stopped her griping.

"Inez can stay, with some conditions," she finally agreed. "She will spend weekends in El Paso and move to *el otro lado* when she's old enough to attend school in the United States."

My bliss ended the day Katalina kept her promise and moved Inez to El Paso.

# III

## 10 KATALINA

**Even now, "what if's" fill my head...**

THE LIGHT OF day makes me cringe. Instead of comforting me from bad dreams, the morning light confirms my nightmare. Ramón kept calling me in my sleep: *Katalina! Katalina!*

The long night started sometime after midnight when the phone rang. I jumped out of bed on the first ring. I had to answer before it woke the children.

"Hello," I whispered, my thumping heart choking me.

"*¿Katalina?*" a man uttered from the other end.

I recognized the voice. It was Alejandro, Ramón's friend.

"*¿Qué quiere?*" I whispered. Why was Alejandro calling? He has to know my husband's in jail.

"You know who I am," Alejandro said.

I remember Ramón introducing me to Alejandro and his brother, Roberto, the first time they visited our home. They were nice but something about them made me nervous. Every time I entered the room, Alejandro stopped the conversation. The brothers returned a couple of times, then they just phoned Ramón. He always left soon after their call.

"What do you want?" I asked.

"*Cuidado*, be careful what you say and who you talk to, someone may be listening to your conversation."

"*¡No llame!*" I snapped.

"All we want is to make sure your family is safe. Ramón knows what to do, and so do you." Alejandro hung up abruptly. What did he mean I know what to do? Will Alejandro listen to me and not call again? I hung up the phone. Sleep escaped me. Hours ticked. Thoughts rushed through my head.

Even now, "what if's" fill my brain. What if Papá Felipe had been sympathetic when I asked to get away from Ramón's infidelity on our third wedding anniversary?

"*Qué vergüenza*," Papá responded. "It would be a disgrace allowing a divorced daughter to live in my home."

Despair forces our hand: Did Papá not understand how desperate I was to ask? What made me think I would find even temporary shelter with my parents?

As I fluff my pillow, an image pops into my head: strings of light illuminating our village town square. It's the night I met Ramón at San Agustin's monthly dance.

Ramón and his family were considered city folk because they came from Torreón. Amalia and her boys had recently moved in with her mother who lived in San Agustin.

At the time of our meeting, Ramón was engaged to the daughter of a prominent family in the village. Nevertheless, he and I gazed at each other like kindred spirits across the square. Two glamorous beings attending the dance as singles. Youthful arrogance—why else would we have ignored Ramón's commitment?

We danced for hours while music poured from cone-shaped speakers. Wood-burning grills cooked *aperitivos*, tasty appetizers washed down with *aguas frescas*, fruit drinks cooled with chunks of ice. A moonlight stroll through the village sustained the illusion. Fantasy faded when we reached the door of my home.

"*¿Cómo es posible?*" Papá hollered, blocking the entrance. "My own daughter making a mockery of me."

Ramón defended me. "Mr. Fuentes, we have done nothing wrong."

"*¡Calle usted!*" Papá scolded. "You have no shame. You are engaged to another woman! What gives you the right to keep *my* daughter out until the early hours of the morning?"

"Papá, it's only twelve o'clock."

"Katalina, have you no pride, tarnishing the reputation of our home?"

Without warning Papá slammed the door.

"*¡Papá, por favor!*" I pleaded.

"Go away, Katalina. Your rebellious behavior is no longer welcome in my home!"

"*¡Perdón, Papá!*" I pleaded for forgiveness. Banging on the door, I screamed for my mother. "*¡Mamá!* Help me! Let me in!"

No one came to the door.

Ramón escorted me to my brother's home, where I stayed until Rodrigo's wife could no longer ignore the uproar in the village.

"People are calling your sister a *mujer perdida*, a fallen woman," she told my brother. "She must leave."

At seventeen, I had no place to go. Yes, I was lost, but not ruined. I'd always protected my virtue, thinking it would protect me. How easily our reputation is tainted when we don't think.

Nothing shocked me anymore—nothing except Ramón's decision to marry me.

"*No es necesario,*" I insisted. "We did nothing wrong."

Deep down inside, I was grateful, desperate, and thrilled.

"What about your studies?" I asked.

"I'll continue them."

Ramón's proposal blinded me. I did not think. If he was unfaithful to others, why wouldn't he be unfaithful to me?

Leaving the past behind in bed, I rise and stretch my body. Lack of sleep makes my joints ache. My head feels drowsy. I consider staying home from work and then remember. My wages, which once supplemented our family income, are now crucial for our existence.

I look in on the kids. Today's Wednesday, two school days left before the weekend. It bothers me to leave the children alone. Someone has always cared for my kids: my in-laws when they were little, and later, housekeepers like Juana.

Pushing my worries aside, I dress for work, then place lunch money for the kids on the kitchen table. Taking a deep breath, I step out the door to face my new world.

A group of *Americanos* and Mexican-American neighbors wait at the bus stop on the corner. The wind carries their whispers: "I saw Mr. Ramirez on the ten o'clock news last night." "Has anyone ever been arrested in our neighborhood before?" "Where did the Ramirez family come from, anyway?"

I wince, detesting public transportation more than ever.

"Good morning," I greet the crowd when I reach the corner.

Some neighbors respond. Others turn away without speaking. You can't blame people for being offended by a family member's deeds, even if you're innocent.

*Maldita suerte*; is it really bad luck or just the result of bad choices?

*Buena suerte*; my luck is changing. Within minutes the bus pulls up to the curb.

### III

THE MORNING LIGHT splashes a pink glow over the Fisher Slacks building. My friend Lupita waits for me by the door.

"Katalina, I saw Ramón on TV last night," she whispers. "*Es cierto*, what they said, is it true?"

"I'll talk to you at lunch." My hurried footsteps do not discourage Lupita. She scurries to keep up with me, following me inside the building.

"You look frazzled," she says.

"*Gracias*, just what I want to hear."

"You may want to get something from the clinic," Lupita suggests.

The doctor at the Fisher Slacks clinic is permitted to prescribe anything the workforce needs for their physical and emotional well-being. Sedatives and amphetamines are handed out with the same ease as aspirin and cough syrup. The blissful escape of sedatives is tempting.

"I'll see you at lunch," I say, deciding against a visit to the clinic. Why be one of many hooked on vices that weaken the human spirit? Best to follow Winston Churchill's advice: "If you are going through hell, keep going." Not easy when every gaze I meet is critical and every smile cynical.

I want to disappear, get away from people. The last person I want to see is Jimmy, but there he is waiting at my machine.

"*Buenos días*," he greets me. "Let me help you with your coat."

I cringe. "Don't touch me!"

Jimmy recoils, his arms and hands hang in the air. He blushes and leaves without speaking.

The bell rings, announcing the start of our workday. I remove my coat and turn on my machine, grateful to have the buzz of equipment drown the whispers.

Guilt grips me for being rude to Jimmy, but he must understand. I'm feeding *la fábrica* enough gossip for a lifetime. Who needs more *chisme*?

Truth is, I can't risk getting close to Jimmy. Right now, the thing I need most is what he offered yesterday: a gentle touch and kindness. Today, that's a dangerous thing.

# III

## 11 INEZ

**Make-believe games get rid of nagging thoughts.**

WHEN I LIVED in Juárez I slept with Abuelita Amalia. In our first El Paso house, I had my own room. I missed snuggling up to Abuelita's warm body, but it was fun having a room to myself, with a real door.

Now, only a curtain separates the kitchen from my tiny bedroom that I had to share with Juana, before the FBI took her away.

This morning I stumble out of bed as soon as Mamá leaves the house. I wash up in the bathroom, trying to forget about yesterday: Papá's arrest, Mamá crying, the phone ringing in the middle of the night. Mamá told whoever called not to call again. Who was she talking to? Was it dad? I've seen them fight, and sometimes Mamá gets pretty mad. Did she tell Papá to go away?

"Mrs. Peel is *never* afraid!" I say to my reflection in the mirror. I tiptoe back to my bedroom, pretending to wear the stiletto heels of the leading lady of *The Avengers* television series.

Make-believe games get rid of nagging thoughts. I came

up with lots of them after Mamá left me behind in Juárez. I still wonder why my parents took only my brothers to live *al otro lado*. Maybe they thought I wouldn't like living on the other side of the border. Or maybe they didn't take me with them because I'm a girl.

Every time I ask Mamá, her answer is the same.

"I had to work," she says.

*Highly illogical!* I want to say, mimicking my favorite new TV character, Mr. Spock.

The whole thing was suspicious. But if they didn't want me, why did they take me to stay with them in El Paso every weekend? If Mamá wanted me with her, why did she forget me in the trolley? It happened the day Papá wasn't around to drive me back to Juárez.

Mamá grabbed Eduardo and Carlitos by the hand when we reached our stop. They left the trolley without me. I shrieked as the doors slammed shut in front of my face.

"You forgot your child!" the driver scolded Mamá. "What's wrong with you?"

Mamá apologized to the man and stared at me quietly. She didn't even tell me she was sorry. Couldn't she see I was scared?

When I was six years old, my parents finally moved me across the border to live with them in the United States. I didn't want to go although I had enjoyed visiting America, especially when Abuelita took us shopping in El Paso.

On shopping day she woke us up early to ride the trolley across the bridge from Mexico to the United States. We'd spend the whole day at the Ropa Usada stores on El Paso Street, Abuelita searching through mounds of used clothing she bought to resell when she traveled back to her village of San Agustin.

Other days, my cousins Jose and Luzita joined me in terrorizing the sales clerks in *la tienda de telas*. We played hide and seek behind cylinders of fabric while Abuelita and Tía Patricia bought new buttons and trims for the clothing.

My parents' home had tile floors and lots of bedrooms, but I wanted to stay in Juárez and play games with my cousins because my brothers never let me play in their games. I cried when my parents told us I was moving to El Paso. Abuelita fainted.

"*¡Mi niña, mi niña!*" my grandmother screeched when she came to. "How can you take my baby to *el otro lado?*"

I didn't understand why I was left behind in the first place, but what really made me mad was Mamá taking me away from my grandmother!

I started having fun in El Paso when I went to school and made friends. Today, I wish it was Saturday so I didn't have to go to school. What will I tell my friends? Maybe I'll walk to school by myself so I don't have to say anything.

What bothers me even more than facing school is that I sent Papá to jail yesterday.

"What am I going to do?" I ask my toy monkey, hugging it to my chest. I hold it out and look at it.

Toy monkey stares back without saying a word.

# III

## 12  INEZ

**Really, what do Mexican hairdressers
know about Twiggy haircuts?**

LAST YEAR WHEN we moved from the valley and I enrolled
at Bowie Elementary, my first friends in my new school were
Linda and Sylvia.

This Wednesday morning, they stand together in the
crowded courtyard of the tall brick building on the hill. The
sun shines and a cool breeze whips around the school. None
of the kids running around in the courtyard seem to mind
the chill. I don't hang out with Linda and Sylvia anymore
but I have to walk past them to reach Laura and our group
of friends.

"Hi, Linda. Hi, Sylvia."

"Hello, Inez!" The girls respond. They do everything
together.

"Cool coats," I say, admiring the matching Mod coats
with fancy velvet collars. I don't mention the lace around their
socks that makes them look like little girls.

"Hey, we're going to the movies on Sunday," Linda says.
"You wanna come?"

"I can't. We visit grandparents on Sunday."

"We'll see you around then." Sylvia drags Linda away.

My old friends don't like my new friends. "Laura and her sisters are cheap girls," Sylvia declared when I started hanging out with Laura. "You know why?"

"Because they don't spend money," I joked.

"No, because their mother divorced their father and married another man."

Linda agreed. "Yeah, that's why the family moved here from wherever they came from. Those girls are trouble. You should stay away from them."

How did Sylvia and Linda know so much about Laura's family? I decided to ignore them because I like hanging out with Laura and her sisters. They're fun to be with, even if Yoli, the oldest sister, taunted me when we first met.

"You still listen to the Beatles?" she asked. "Don't you know the Beatles are dead? James Brown, he's the man—*the King of Soul*! Besides, the Beatles play stomper music."

"What is soul?" I asked. "And what does stomper mean?"

"Stompers are *gringos* who dance funny," Laura explained.

I roared with laughter when Laura stomped the floor to demonstrate.

"And this is *soul*!" Yoli dropped the turntable needle on a record. James Brown's voice came screeching through the speakers.

"Let's do the jerk!" Liz hollered, jerking her short body until her wavy hair fell over her face.

It's hard to believe Liz and Laura are twins. Liz is short and chubby, and her short wavy hair almost looks blonde. Laura has long dark hair and her long legs make her look like a baby giraffe learning to walk at birth.

This morning, Liz is her usual sassy self. "Why do you

bother with the snob sisters?" she asks when I join the group of girls.

"Sylvia and Linda aren't sisters," Laura says. "They're just snobs."

Everyone laughs except me.

"Those socks your friends wear make them look like fucking kids." Mona, one of the trendiest girls in school, puts down my old friends.

I'm not sure I like Mona although I *love* her Twiggy haircut. When I begged Mamá for the same cut, she had no idea what I was talking about.

"Twiggy!" I said, pointing to a picture of the English fashion model.

Mamá agreed but insisted on using her hairdresser in Juárez.

"Why can't we use someone in El Paso?" I grumbled. Really, what do Mexican hairdressers know about Twiggy haircuts?

Sure enough, the stylist botched it, then claimed my thick hair didn't work with the style.

"Why didn't she say that before?" I snapped when we left the shop. "I hate it!"

"*¡No seas necia!*" Mamá chided. "Stop being a brat. Your hair will grow back."

My hair hasn't grown an inch since that day. I run my fingers through it while Mona checks out my outfit. She points at the fishnet stockings I'm wearing with a pinstriped skirt and oversized shirt.

"Nice stockings," she says.

I'm flattered. "Thanks, but they're tights, not stockings."

"Yeah, okay, " Mona mutters.

Our conversation is interrupted when the school bell rings announcing class. Everyone scatters.

"Where were you this morning?" Laura asks as we enter our homeroom. "We waited—"

"Running late," I interrupt.

"I know, but why?"

"Not feeling well," I lie. What am I supposed to say—dad was arrested last night?

"I figured something was up because you're never late."

Two students chase each other across the room. The class is rowdy because our homeroom teacher hasn't arrived yet.

"Inez! Why is that creep staring at you?" Laura gestures toward my neighbor Lalo. He's sitting alone at one of the square tables grouped together for art projects.

"Just ignore him," I say, sitting down at my desk. Laura ignores me.

"What you looking at, fucking *joto*!" she screams.

The class laughs when she calls Lalo a faggot. He glares back without responding.

Our teacher Mrs. Rogers arrives. She's young, has a pretty face, and wears nice clothes, but Mamá says those things don't matter if you're fat.

Following Mrs. Rogers is the tallest boy in class, Ricardo. He dashes across the floor and sits beside me. His long legs barely fit under the desk.

"Richard, your persistent tardiness must stop!" Mrs. Rogers demands.

"Please, Miss, my name is *Ricardo*, not Richard, Ritchie, or Ricky. It's *Ricardo*."

"And my name is *Mrs.* Rogers," the teacher sniffs. "Ree-car-do, not only are you disruptive, but you're insolent.

Perhaps we should take a walk to Mr. Brady's office and see what the principal has to say."

"Oh, Miss, I'm only two minutes late and I did not mean to be *insolent*."

The class chuckles at Ricardo and his mocking tone.

"What does insolent mean?" a student asks.

"The word means rude, disrespectful!" Mrs. Rogers declares. She looks like she's counting to ten. Maybe she remembers that she was late herself. "Okay, Ree-car-do, you get one more chance!"

"Thank you, ma'am," Ricardo chuckles.

I want to be insolent and tell the teacher my name is pronounced *E*-nez not *I*-nez, but I don't. Mrs. Rogers turns her attention to the class.

"Students, today I'd like to discuss a matter about to be settled in our city. It's a dispute that started in 1910."

"That's a long time to be mad," Ricardo says. The class laughs.

"Ree-car-do, please raise your hand if you want to comment. Now, can someone tell me, what is the Treaty of Guadalupe Hidalgo about and why is it so important?"

Lalo is the only student to raise his hand. "The treaty ended the Mexican-American War."

"Correct! The United States and Mexico signed the Treaty of Guadalupe Hidalgo on February 2, 1848. On that day, the Mexican government surrendered to the United States the territories that would become the states of New Mexico, Texas, Utah, California, Colorado, Arizona, and Nevada. And the Mexican residents of these territories became Americans."

When I was in fifth grade, Papá took me to the Federal Courthouse to become an American.

"Why?" I asked him.

"You must become a *ciudadana Americana*," he said, smiling. "Without papers you're a *mojada*. An undocumented Mexican is an illegal, and we can't have that."

I worried. *Mojada* means wetback and kids teased you with that word all the time.

"How come I'm not an American citizen already?"

"Because your mother wanted Amá Lucia to be the one to deliver you when you were born. Since your great-grandmother can't come to the United States, Katalina went to Mexico."

At the courthouse, a man told me to recite the Pledge of Allegiance. I knew it by heart because I learned it in the first grade.

"Congratulations, Inez, you are now an American," the man said.

"I thought living in America made me an American," I said.

"You're lucky your mama was born in this country," the man said, chuckling.

"All that land belonged to Mexico?" Ricardo asks.

"Yes, Ree-car-do. The Treaty of Guadalupe Hidalgo also designated the middle of the Rio Grande as the international boundary between the United States and Mexico, but sometime between 1852 and 1864, the river shifted south, and a flood relocated about six hundred acres onto the side of the United States."

"Who cares," Laura mutters under her breath.

"Laura, did you want to say something?"

"No, ma'am."

"Then stop mumbling!" Mrs. Rogers continues talking

as she walks toward the other end of the room. "The Hidalgo Treaty set the boundary between the countries down the middle of the river and any amendment had to result from natural causes, such as erosion, or material deposited by running water."

Laura's right. This information can put you to sleep. Mrs. Rogers keeps talking, "There were no prearrangements for land cut off by floods or sudden changes in the river's course. This unexpected development led the Mexican government to act on behalf of Mexican property-owners and file a claim against the United States."

"Mexico stayed quiet until now?" Ricardo asks.

"No. The International Boundary Commission, established in 1889, reviewed the case. It included representatives from Mexico, the United States, and Canada. A decision was made to divide the parcel known as the Chamiza Thicket between Mexico and the United States, but the Mexican government challenged the verdict. It's taken over fifty years to settle the matter."

"How much land are we talking about, Miss?"

"Ree-car-do, please raise your hand." Mrs. Rogers sighs before continuing. "It's a small tract of land, some four hundred acres, about two hundred less than the original claim. It also includes almost four hundred structures."

Ricardo's hand goes up.

Mrs. Rogers smiles. "Yes?"

"So what do we get from this deal?"

"Mostly good will. The United States receives payment for the structures, but both countries share the cost of rechanneling the river."

The teacher gestures to Sheldon, one of two white boys in our class.

"How do you rechannel a river?"

"I don't know, Sheldon, but we're about to find out. The work starts as soon as President Johnson and Mexican President Ordaz sign the formal settlement."

"It's a long time to be mad," Ricardo repeats.

The class laughs again.

I remember when Tía Chayo took me to see President Johnson and *Presidente* Ordaz the first time the United States and Mexican presidents met in El Paso. I was so excited—until I fainted. The hot weather caused other people to faint too, but Carlitos teased me about it all summer.

"All right, class, that's your history lesson for today," Mrs. Rogers announces. "Let's get our art projects from the shelves and see if we can finish them today."

Ricardo smiles at me as we get up. Liz says he's got a crush on me.

"But no one dates cripples even when they're cute like Ricardo," Liz taunted.

Sometimes I hate the things my friends say. Last year, Ricardo was in a serious car crash. The doctors saved his arm but he lost the use of his hand. I wonder if I'd go out with a boy who has a messed-up hand.

"Pay attention, students," Mrs. Rogers says when the bell rings. "All projects are due tomorrow. If you finished today, leave your work on my desk."

I pass Lalo on my way out.

"How is your family today?" he sneers.

I know Lalo's talking about what happened at my house yesterday.

"Why is he asking about your family?" Laura asks when I join her in the hallway.

"Who knows? Maybe he's a fucking jerk!"

"Holy shit," Laura giggles. "You never curse!"

My cursing startles me too. My parents don't allow it. We can't even use slang words. "Only common people curse," Mamá warned.

"Who cares?" I say aloud.

"Who cares about what?" Laura looks surprised.

"Who cares what anyone has to say?" I rush off to our next class.

# III

## 13 KATALINA

**Without warning resentment rises inside me.**

MY BODY TREMBLES when the music stops, and my name comes roaring through the speakers: "Katalina Ramirez, please report to the office. Katalina Ramirez to the office."

It isn't possible, yet I'm convinced production at Fisher Slacks Manufacturing stops. Employees stare and whisper, taunting me as I rush through the aisles of equipment: "Did you see Katalina's husband in the news last night? Busted for selling marijuana! Miss Precious married to a pusher!"

There is no such thing as innocent until proven guilty, not in the court of everyday people. The harshest penalty is reserved for someone we think witnessed a crime and did nothing to stop it. I have been found guilty of the crime of poor judgment by a jury of my peers made up of Fisher Slacks employees.

I burst into the office. Josie the office manager sits behind one of two desks facing each other. She motions to the desk across from hers.

"Sit down, honey. Your husband's on the phone."

"*Tú esposo*," her assistant says.

"Ramón?" Without hesitation I pick up the receiver. "Hello? Hello?"

Josie leans over and pushes a flashing button.

"*¿Katalina?*" Ramón sounds rushed and anxious.

"*Si.*" I sit up in the chair. "Where are you?"

"I can't go into details. A lawyer was just assigned to my case. His name is Ralph Torres. He'll call you tonight. Take down his telephone number in case you miss him."

Borrowing a pencil and paper, I prepare to write down the information.

"Go ahead."

Ramón recites the number and adds, "He'll call you at six o'clock to explain everything."

"*¿Qué va pasar?*" I ask, knowing neither of us can predict the future.

"*No sé.* I have to go. Make sure you're home to take the call."

"*¡Ramón!*" The dial tone pierces my ear.

"Are you all right, honey?" Josie asks. "Your face is whiter than a sheet."

"I'm fine. Thank you." I hang up the receiver.

"It sounds like your husband's in hot water, honey."

"*Cuídate.*" Josie's assistant tries to comfort me. "Take care of yourself." She returns to her desk when I get up.

With a nod of appreciation, I leave the office. Fear grips me. I need to calm my nerves. I trudge down the hall to the bathroom.

The room is so quiet, it feels as if I'm the only one occupying the facility. A whiff of cheap perfume tells me I'm wrong. A toilet flushes and Angelina steps out from a stall. This woman hates me for reasons unknown, but her taunts need an audience and we're alone. I ignore her on my way inside a stall. Through the crack between the hinges of the door, I see Angelina chewing gum. She fluffs her hair, blows a bubble, and mumbles, "*Sangrona.*" Angelina insists I'm a snob.

Easing out of the stall, I walk to the sink and moisten a paper towel. The cool paper remains on my forehead until the lunch bell rings.

|||

IN THE NOISY cafeteria, Lupita greets me with flailing arms, drawing attention to my arrival. No use cowering. I lift my head and stride toward her table.

"*¿Por qué te llamaron?*" Lupita wants to know why I was called into the office. She takes a bite of her burrito and sits ready to listen.

The smell of food, people gawking and whispering—all of it makes me nauseous. Lupita agrees to leave the lunchroom. She takes another bite of food before wrapping up her burrito. Food is not permitted on the manufacturing floor.

We finally leave the cafeteria and make our way to Lupita's machine, where we huddle whispering.

"It was Ramón. Thank God. It was torture not knowing anything."

"*¿No sabías?*" Lupita sounds surprised. "You didn't know… where he was?"

"I knew nothing."

Lupita whispers, "The newscast said Ramón had been under surveillance."

"*Sospeche.* Ramón denied my suspicions. When Inez told me FBI agents had searched our home—"

"Inez?"

"The FBI was searching the house when she got home from school yesterday afternoon. They told her Ramón had been arrested. The agents took Juana and left Inez alone."

"*¡Malditos!* Only men trained by Hoover would leave a little girl by herself."

I imagine Inez, her frightened face when she encountered strangers searching her home. And then she was left alone. My body quivers.

"J. Edgar Hoover, *dictator* of the FBI," Lupita rages, "breaks all the rules and doesn't have much use for people of color. He even disrespected the Kennedys. The guy is ruthless, *inhumano!*"

Guilt washes over me. I'm ashamed not to have considered Inez's feelings. I must speak to my daughter. It's better to say anything than nothing at all.

"So what did Ramón say?" Lupita asks.

Lupita's question stops me from fretting about Inez. "What?" I ask impatiently.

"Ramón—what did he say?"

"He said his lawyer's calling to explain everything. Maybe he'll tell me how I'm supposed to pay for his services."

"Ramón left no money?"

"*Nada.* Not a dime."

"*¿Cómo?* He must have made money."

Is Lupita judging me, skeptical like everyone around here? Ramón is a master at making money, he just can't keep it. I don't mention that to my friend, instead I snap.

"Do you think I'd be working here if..."

"You poor thing," Lupita says with a sympathetic look.

It's degrading to be perceived as pitiful. I know what

Lupita is thinking and she's probably right. Ramón invested in a tavern and purchased a car. I'm sure he spent the rest of his money on other women.

The bell signals the end of the lunch break.

"Call me if you need anything," Lupita says before leaving.

Like clockwork, the buzz of equipment and music fills the building.

I don't recall the walk to my workstation, but suddenly I'm there starting my machine. My foot slams down on the lever. Without warning resentment rises inside me.

My husband is being cared for, even has an attorney who will explain everything, while I tend to the kids by myself, alone!

The lump in my throat almost chokes me. *Egoísta*, thinking only of myself.

# III

## 14 RAMÓN

**Don't bring my family into this!**

MY ATTORNEY, RALPH Torres, stands in front of the small table between our seats. He glances at the gold watch glimmering against his dark skin as I hang up the phone after talking to Katalina. "You should leave if you have somewhere to be," I tell him.

"Ramón, why didn't you tell me you hadn't called your wife? The agents read you your rights, correct?"

A fan buzzes overhead.

"*Sí, Señor Torres,*" I say, lighting another cigarette. I sit back in my chair at the small table and stare up at him. Truth is, I wasn't looking forward to speaking with Katalina. I couldn't even bring myself to ask how she and the kids are doing.

"Please call me Ralph. Did you understand them, your rights?"

"*Seguro,* yes, of course I understood them."

"Ramón, from now on we will only converse in English. If they put you on the stand when we go to trial, I need you to feel comfortable speaking the language. *¿Comprende?*"

I nod.

"They almost violated your rights by not allowing you a phone call within twenty-four hours of your arrest." The attorney finishes taking out papers from his briefcase. He removes his jacket and sits down. "All right, Ramón, let's go over this again. According to your file, you were arrested at the Paso del Norte Bridge. The FBI has established your connection to Miguel, who was driving the truck loaded with fifty kilos of marijuana across the border. They also connected you to Roberto, who was arrested at the El Paso Greyhound Bus Terminal for attempting to ship thirty kilos of the same narcotic to Chicago. Your telephone has been under surveillance and your Mustang confiscated as evidence. The only one who got away was Roberto's brother, Alejandro, and the only way to beat this thing is for you to cut a deal with the prosecutor."

"What do you mean? Turn in Alejandro?"

"Roberto is not turning in his brother, and Miguel is too low on the food chain to know much. Give me some names and I'll have you out by tomorrow."

Ralph's comments resemble the FBI agents' and his arrogance reminds me of Alejandro.

I had met Alejandro and Roberto before, but we became pals the day the bank foreclosed on my house. Kiko's Bar offered the false courage I needed to face my wife and family. After a couple of drinks, I headed to the men's bathroom. On the way out, Alejandro pulled me aside and invited me to join him and his brother.

"You know we moved to El Paso from Chicago to start a business," Alejandro said.

"You haven't told me yet what kind of business."

Roberto's high-pitched cackle caused patrons to turn and stare.

"I can't go into details but our business will take us into Mexico," Alejandro said.

That night I received money to relocate my family to a new home. A few weeks later, Roberto called saying Alejandro wanted me to make arrangements for our first trip together into Mexico.

Now my attorney is asking me to snitch on these people.

"I can't turn anyone in," I tell Ralph Torres. I can't risk the fate Alejandro's associate endured, let alone putting my family in danger. Alejandro had made this venture sound so simple. "Kids out in California are smoking weed like cigarettes," he said chuckling, "All we have to do is deliver it." Supply and demand. The only risk? The product was illegal.

"Listen, Ramón, you're not fighting a traffic ticket. This crime carries heavy penalties, and you're not giving me anything to work with. The only thing I can argue is that your participation in the organization was so minimal you couldn't even secure the financial future of your family."

"*¡Basta!* Don't bring my family into this!"

"*You* brought them into this yourself, Ramón. I'm just trying to help. I'm going in front of a judge for your bail hearing. This is your first offense. You're not charged with possession, and I'm in a good position to negotiate, but we're still looking at a couple of thousand dollars to get you out of here. Does your wife have that kind of money?"

When I don't answer Ralph starts packing the paperwork spread out on the table. "Ramón, I've been practicing law for ten years. Let me share my experience. I've faced people who are convinced Mexicans lack the intellect to practice law. Fortunately, there are others with better reasoning, but sometimes people who offer opportunity don't like it when you disappoint them. And then you have good old institutional racism, and that's as powerful as the legal system. I like to win and will do whatever it takes to succeed, but there are limitations."

I draw hard on my cigarette, recalling all the times *los Americanos* confused my accent for a lack of intellect, dismissing me rather than asking me to repeat my words. "I know about limitations," I say.

The attorney stands from the table and locks his briefcase.

"I have to leave, Ramón. Think about what we discussed, and tell me what you want to do. If you're found guilty, you may get the maximum sentence. Fifteen to twenty years is a long time to be in prison."

"I don't have to think about it. I won't cooperate with the authorities."

"It's your nickel, Ramón. I'll be in touch." The attorney puts on his jacket and leaves.

Ralph Torres is right. I've made a mess of things, but I know one thing. Silence is the only protection I can afford for my family.

# III

## 15  INEZ

**"So you would never go out with John Lennon?"**

IN MY DREAMS, I kissed Ricky Nelson. It happened after he sang on the Ozzie and Harriet TV show. It felt so good, I woke up embarrassed. When my boyfriend Johnny tried to kiss me, I wouldn't let him.

"You better let me kiss you, Inez, or I'll find another girl."

Johnny found a new girl.

I still think kissing is disgusting. As far as kissing a white boy in my dreams—of course I kept *that* to myself. Mamá would never approve. She's always telling stories about *los Americanos*, like how they didn't allow her and Papá to eat at a restaurant.

"Maybe it was the way you were dressed," Carlitos argued.

"Bigotry has nothing to do with fashion," Mamá responded.

I have no idea what the word "bigotry" means, but it sounded ugly when Mamá said it.

My math teacher's voice interrupts my daydream, returning me to class.

"Come on, Sheldon, you're a smart boy. Now let's try it again."

The class applauds when Sheldon solves the fractions on the blackboard. He looks in my direction, his mouth forming words without making a sound: "You're next."

I blush, shaking my head.

Fortunately, the lunch bell rings before it's my turn. The teacher dismisses the class. Laura turns to look at me as we make our way down the hallway.

"What's wrong with you?" Laura asks. "You look dazed."

Sheldon walks between us, bumping against me as he passes.

"Excuse me, gotta move or you'll get hurt!" Sheldon dashes away, chuckling.

"Hey!" I holler.

"He likes you," Laura chants.

"Yeah, right. In case you haven't noticed, Sheldon is a *gringo*."

"So you would never go out with John Lennon?"

"Would you go out with James Brown?"

"Hey, can you imagine kissing a colored boy or a *gringo*?"

"E-e-e-e-u-w!" We screech and run down the hallway.

### III

THE SMELL OF milk and scorched food creeps through the lunch room but the hot dog and fries on my plate are tasty. Everyone at the table has a plate in front of them, except Mona. She keeps picking food from everyone's plate.

"So who's going to Carol's party this Saturday?" Liz asks.

"Me!" several girls scream.

"What are you wearing?" Liz asks Mona.

"I'm borrowing a dress from Maria."

"You're allowed to borrow clothes from friends?" I ask.

"Yeah, something wrong with that?" Mona snaps.

"I'm not allowed to borrow clothes, even from relatives."

"Why, you got cooties or something?" Mona's remark makes the girls laugh and makes me feel like a jerk. "Are you going to the party?" She grabs a French fry from my plate.

"I don't think so."

"Why not?" Mona stares at me.

I remember Papá telling me about going to parties.

"You have to be selective so people think you're special," he said.

"But how can you be special if people don't know you exist?" I insisted.

Papá smiled without answering my question.

"My father thinks I'm too young to be out at night by myself," I tell Mona.

"Your dad's a fool!"

The girls gasp. Parents don't make sense, but they're always respected. I want to slap Mona across the face. Instead, I slide my empty plate toward her.

"Stop picking from everyone's plate," I say. "Go get seconds."

Mona rushes off with my plate.

"You know she spends her lunch money on cigarettes and makeup," Liz says.

"That's not true," one of the other girls explains. "Mona's dad left the family, and her mother can't afford lunch money. Mona won't bring the sandwiches her mother makes for her."

"Yeah, okay." Laura mimics Mona.

The girls laugh but I'm still mad. Mona is a rude girl.

### |||

AFTER LUNCH, WE pass a group of boys sitting by the exit to the lunchroom. One of them is Nicky. He's friendly to everyone, but rumor has it he and Mona are more than friends. Nicky smiles at Mona and then turns to me.

"Hey, Inez, have you heard this new band called The Doors?"

"Nope."

"You must," he insists.

"I will."

Nicky chuckles. Mona huffs and stomps off. We follow her to the courtyard.

The midday sun has warmed the day and rid the yard of shadows. We form a circle to wait out the remainder of the lunch break.

"Hey, you guys wanna hang out after school?" Mona asks.

"Hang out where?" Liz wants to know.

"Five Points. We can go to Sears and Woolworth's, check out stuff."

"We'll go. How about you, Inez?" Laura asks.

"I can't," I mumble.

"Is there anything you *can* do?" Mona asks, sneering at me. *"Anything?"*

My face flushes. Part of me wants to tell the girls what happened yesterday at my house. I walk away, listening to Mona's words: "What's up with *her*? Inez thinks she's so special."

What did I do to make Mona mad? She's the one being

rude. Laura catches up to me, and we walk back to our class-room together.

"So are you hanging out after school?" I ask.

"Yeah, Ma's working and Beto doesn't care." Laura's step-dad Beto is supposed to be in charge when their mother is at work.

"Why are you friends with Mona? She's so mean and nasty!"

"She's Liz's friend, not mine."

In class I stare out the window, trying to understand feel-ings I can't explain. It was always easy ignoring people who made me feel bad. Now, they make me mad. I hate Mona for embarrassing me in front of my friends, and I hate Lalo for teasing about Papá. Most of all, I'm mad at myself for not protecting my dad.

For the first time ever I don't want to go home. After what happened yesterday, I don't know what to expect. Mona is a jerk, but I still want to hang out with the girls. Better than going home and getting hassled. Laura's sister Yoli taught us two new words: hassled and pissed off.

Right now, I'm pretty pissed off and I don't want to be hassled!

# III

## 16  INEZ

**"Dios mío, his own son calling his father a criminal!"**

WE ALL NEED someone who makes us smile. Someone who makes us feel so special the corners of our mouth curve up without trying. Someone who sprinkles stardust on bad days and makes us forget all about them. For me, that special some-one is Abuelita Amalia.

I'm thrilled to find her sitting on the porch steps with Tía Patricia and Tío Emilio when my brothers and I arrive home from school. What a difference from yesterday when I found strangers in my house.

I run and hug Abuelita, kissing her cheek. When we're together, it feels like no one else is around us.

"*¡Inez mi'ja!*" Abuelita clutches me and whispers in my ear, "*Pajarito.*" Little bird is her pet name for me. I tighten my grip on her.

Carlitos gives me a dirty look. He's always telling me Abuelita spoils me. Today, I ignore him. Eduardo unlocks the door. Our grandmother releases me and turns to face my brothers.

"*Sus abuelos* send their love," she says.

My brothers respond with a nod to Amá and Abuelo Sabino's message. Lately, Eduardo and Carlitos act as if they're too cool to care about people they love.

Abuelita wants to know if we're hungry.

"*¡Si, señora!*" we respond eagerly.

The boys and Tío Emilio sit down to watch TV. I follow the women into the kitchen. There are so many special moments I shared with the Ramirez women when I lived with the family in Juárez. Great-grandmother Lucia taught me embroidery. That was a special occasion because Amá, who prefers that name to *Bisabuela*, great-grandmother, hardly ever bothers with kids unless she's disciplining us.

"*Paciencia, Inez,*" she warned. "This work requires patience and diligence. You can't be sloppy with it." Amá unraveled my first stitching. "Redo it until you master the skill."

One Christmas Eve, Tía Patricia taught me to make *atole.* "You can't have a *Nochebuena* without *tamales* and *atole.* Bring me one of those *piloncillos* and I'll show you how to make one of my favorite drinks."

I grabbed one of the brown sugar cones and handed it to Tía Patricia. She took *el piloncillo* and added the brown sugar to the hot water she was thickening with *masa.* After she seasoned the corn meal with *canela,* the fresh cinnamon made the *atole* as tasty as hot chocolate.

Another exciting time was El Día de los Muertos festivities. Abuelita created wreaths, which we spent days decorating with papier-mâché and flowers. When El Día arrived, we packed a picnic lunch and headed to the cemetery to celebrate the departed.

The ritual I enjoyed most took place every weeknight. Once the family was fed and the kitchen cleaned, the women sat around the radio. The room grew quiet as they listened to the wicked lives of the characters on their favorite soap operas, *las novelas*.

Abuelita mended garments, Tía Patricia pressed laundry, and Amá Lucia prayed with her rosary beads. I stayed under the covers in the bed I shared with Abuelita in a corner of the room. No one spoke until the commercial break.

"*Hortensia es babosa.*" Abuelita was always the first to comment.

"*¡No!*" Tía Patricia defended. "Hortensia is not a silly woman. She's in love with Pedro and Dario."

"*¡Esa mujer es puta!*" Amá Lucia argued. "You can't love two men and be decent! That woman is a whore." Amá quietly returned to her prayer beads.

Once the *novelas* were over, Abuelita joined me in bed. We snuggled until I fell asleep to the night sounds of the house: the ticking of the windup clock, the crackle of a burning candle. Bed springs squeaked and snores roared until the night gently surfaced as morning.

Today, Abuelita stands by the stove, watching me sitting at the kitchen table.

"How are you, *mi'ja*?" she asks.

For the first time ever, I'm not honest with my grandmother. "*Bien,*" I lie.

Abuelita always seems to know what I'm thinking or feeling. She gestures to Tía Patricia who steps up to the stove and takes over the cooking.

"*Venté conmigo,*" Abuelita says, hugging me from behind. "Come stay with us. It's been a while since you spent a weekend in Juárez."

"*No puedo,* I have a lot of schoolwork." I turn around and

wrap my arms around Abuelita's belly, wishing I could tell her everything that's bugging me. But how can I share my feelings about snitching on my father? And what do abuelitas know about girls like Mona? Sometimes it's best just to keep quiet.

III

THE AROMA OF *papas con chorizo* still lingers when Mamá walks into the kitchen. I'm finishing the meal of potatoes and sausage with my brothers and Tío Emilio. Abuelita starts weeping as soon as she sees Mamá.

Tía Patricia offers a plate of food to Mamá. "*Venté a comer.*"

"*No gracias*, but thank you for feeding the kids."

No one says anything about Abuelita's tears. I hate when the family ignores her feelings. Don't they know how sensitive she is?

"How are you?" Mamá finally asks Abuelita.

"*Corazón espinado.*" Abuelita says, drying her tears. "Thorns pierce my heart like they wound *El Sagrado Corazón.*" Abuelita pauses to light a cigarette. "My son—have you heard from him since his arrest yesterday?"

Mamá removes a bottle of aspirin from one of the cupboards and walks to the sink to fetch a glass of water.

"Ramón called this morning," Mamá says before swallowing the pill.

"*¡Gracias a Dios!* How is he?"

"His attorney is supposed to call me at six o'clock."

"He has an attorney?" Tío Emilio sounds surprised.

"God only knows how I'm paying for his service."

Eduardo pipes up. "The court appoints free attorneys to criminals."

"*¿Criminal?*" Abuelita starts weeping again. "*Dios mío*, his own son calling his father a criminal."

"*¡Eduardo, por favor!*" Mamá scolds my brother, then turns to Abuelita. "He didn't mean his father."

I close my eyes. Two things we can count on when our families meet: Abuelita's tears and a fight between her and Mamá.

Eduardo explains his class is studying the Supreme Court in school. He recites his lesson: "In 1963 the Supreme Court determined that the Constitution required state courts to provide attorneys if the person charged with a crime could not afford a lawyer."

"They only passed the law four years ago?" Carlitos asks in English. "So how did people defend themselves before 1963?"

"*¡Niños!*" Mamá chides, falling into a chair. "How many times must I tell you it's rude to speak a language other people don't understand? Go watch TV!"

My brothers dash out of the kitchen. I trail behind. Does Mamá know we're not allowed to speak Spanish in school? And even if we could, who wants to sound like their parents?

# III

## 17 KATALINA

**Children's resilience soothes the soul and breaks the heart.**

PATRICIA'S COOKING REMINDS me of life with the Ramirez family in Mexico. At times Patricia and I supported each other against Amalia's bullying. Usually Patricia sided with Amalia. The day Ramón insisted on moving to *la frontera*, I couldn't wait to go. So why is the presence of the Ramirez family so comforting today?

I feel sorry for Amalia. *Sea lo que sea*; whatever her faults, no mother deserves to see her son in jail.

"What kind of service can an attorney provide for free?" Emilio persists.

Eduardo's speech eased my tension. Now, Emilio's remark annoys me.

"Any legal advice will help Ramón."

Emilio looks as if he wants to argue. He lights a cigarette as the phone rings.

"I'll get it!" I scream in the direction of the kids. The clock on the wall reads exactly six o'clock. "Hello?" I whisper.

"*¿Señora Ramirez?*" The voice on the other end speaks

perfect Spanish. "This is Ralph Torres. I'm representing your husband."

"When can I see Ramón?"

The attorney stutters as if I startled him. "Mrs. Ramirez… the county jail's visiting hours are Fridays at three, but it's urgent that you and I meet. A federal grand jury just indicted your husband. Bail was set at five thousand dollars. The evidence is overwhelming."

My racing heart makes it difficult to speak.

"*¿Señora Ramirez?*"

"So much money… When can we meet?"

"Today is Wednesday…. How about tomorrow at six o'clock? My office is located on Magoffin Avenue."

I write down the attorney's address. "I'll be there."

"I look forward to meeting you, *Señora* Ramirez."

Without saying goodbye, I hang up the phone and leave the kitchen.

Amalia's weeping fades as I shut myself behind the bathroom door. Five thousand dollars! I make thirty dollars a week. How long will it take to earn that amount? I splash cold water on my face and grab a towel to dry it.

On the way back to the kitchen, I fetch a pack of Lucky Strikes from my dresser. I light a cigarette while sitting down at the table.

"Ramón won't be coming home soon," I announce.

"*¿Por qué?*" Amalia demands.

"Because I don't have five thousand dollars for his bail! Do you?"

Amalia starts sobbing hysterically. "*¡Dios!* Save me from this misery Lord."

Patricia finishes washing the dishes and walks to the stove.

"We could all use a cup of coffee," she says.

"I have to sell Ramón's business in Juárez," I say. The tavern was a suspicious investment and a source of spats between Ramón and me. It's even more upsetting now, knowing it was purchased with illegal money. Still, its sale will benefit my family.

"Why sell the *cantina*?" Emilio asks.

"To free your brother." I'm growing impatient. Doesn't Emilio understand it's the only way to raise money for Ramón's bail? I crush my cigarette in the ashtray. Sometimes it's difficult to believe Ramón and Emilio are brothers. My husband's not only good-looking with a sense of style, Ramón possesses a more generous nature.

Emilio has some nasty habits I can't dismiss. Several housekeepers have complained about my brother-in-law arriving unannounced, making sure we're not home so he can snoop through the furniture and closets.

"Emilio, why don't we meet in Juárez and start looking for a buyer?" I suggest. In Mexico, it's still taboo for women to engage in any way with taverns. It will be difficult to seek a buyer by myself.

"I'll deal with this myself," Emilio says. "You have to work."

It takes me a minute to realize why Emilio wants to take care of the tavern. The Ramirez family still operates as a hierarchy. If Ramón's in prison, Emilio will be expected to look after his family, and that means getting access to our money.

"*¡Vámonos!*" Emilio abruptly instructs his wife and mother. He stands. "We better get going."

In the living room, the kids are mesmerized by a report on TV. A man is talking about something called a sit-in.

"Young rebels, described as hippies, perform a sit-in outside San Francisco's City Hall." The camera follows the reporter toward a group of girls with flowers in their hair and young men wearing headbands. The crowd sits on the granite steps of the building, blocking three glass doors framed with elaborate gilt trim. The reporter continues: "These young people are challenging the policies of our government and the conventional lifestyles of their parents."

"*Despídanse,*" I say, instructing my children to say goodbye to their relatives.

The kids don't move. Instead they chant in unison: "Bye!"

"Bye?" Amalia whimpers. "What does that word mean?"

Inez walks over and kisses her grandmother's cheek, but it's too late. Amalia makes no effort to hold back her tears. I turn off the TV and gesture to Eduardo and Carlitos. They walk over and give their grandmother a good-bye kiss.

Amalia's spirits are lifted. She leaves the house smiling.

I peer at the family through the window. Amalia and Patricia wear the same rustic scarves they wore in San Agustin. With their modest clothing and headgear, the Ramirez women always stand out in our neighborhood.

"Mamá," Eduardo calls out, "are we getting the Mustang back?"

"*No sé,* but I'll find out when I visit the attorney."

Children's resilience soothes the soul and breaks the heart with one blow.

# III

## 18 INEZ

**What a blast, cruising with the Beach Boys blaring "Good Vibrations" through the windows.**

I GET EDUARDO'S QUESTION about the Mustang. Ever since my brother got his driver's permit he wants to get behind the wheel of any car. But the Ford Mustang is special with its bold white curves and black leather interior. Every year, Papá came home with a new automobile: Bel Airs, Impalas; none came close to the Mustang. It's the coolest car we ever had.

The first time Papá let Eduardo drive it, my brother complained about having to take me along.

"Inez goes or no one rides it." Papá held the keys until Eduardo agreed.

Who cares if I have to squeeze in the back seat with Carlitos? What a blast, cruising the neighborhood with the Beach Boys blaring "Good Vibrations" through the windows. I can't wait to learn to drive!

When Abuelita's family leaves, Mamá gestures to me. I follow her into the kitchen. Since Juana left, it's my duty to clean up after dinner. What a hassle!

I smell the cigarettes but to my surprise someone washed the dirty dishes.

"I wanted you to see what Tía Patricia did for you," Mamá says as the phone starts ringing. "You can thank her next time you see her."

I jump to pick up the receiver.

"Hello?"

"Inez, it's your Tía." Mamá's younger sister always sounds like she drinks too much caffeine. "Please let me speak with your mother."

"Hello, Tía Chayo." Before I can pass the phone, Mamá grabs the receiver and brushes me aside. "You're welcome," I say, stomping into my room.

The curtain over the doorway doesn't block Tía Chayo's voice as it spills from the receiver: "*Padre mío,* is it true Ramón was on television?"

"I was about to call you." Mamá sits down at the kitchen table before continuing. "I'm meeting his attorney tomorrow and we're visiting Ramón this Friday."

Tía Chayo's voice drifts in and out. Sprawling on the bed, I cover my head with a pillow hoping it will block out Mamá's chatter. It doesn't.

"Thank you, but Amalia and the family are going with us. They just left. Will you be at church on Sunday?"

There is silence as Mamá listens.

"I've never been through anything like this before. How should I know what's going to happen?"

"Leave it to Ramón!" Tía Chayo's voice comes through loud and clear.

"*¡Por favor!*" Mamá chides her little sister. "I'm in no

mood for critics. I'll see you at church on Sunday." Mamá listens. "*Gracias,*" she says and hangs up.

I hear her light a cigarette. Suddenly, the phone rings again.

"Hello!" Mamá snaps into the receiver. "Laura?"

I jump up and dash into the kitchen. Mamá has her back to me.

"Hold on, I think Inez went to bed."

I snatch the receiver and deliberately push Mamá aside—see how she likes the feeling.

"Laura?"

"Hi, Inez, were you already in bed?"

"No."

"Well, that's what your mom said!"

"Well, she's wrong." I glare at my mother.

Mamá frowns and shakes her head before leaving the kitchen.

"So what are you doing?" Laura asks.

"Watching *The Monkees,*" I fib.

"You watch *The Monkees?*"

Darn, why did I pick such a stupid show? "So what's up?"

"Did you ask your mother about going to Carol's party on Saturday?"

"Not yet."

"What are you waiting for?"

"It's only Wednesday. Besides I don't think I want to go." I'm still pissed about Mona's comment that my father is foolish for not allowing me to go to parties.

"Too bad, because we got some new makeup we're wearing to the party."

"You bought makeup?"

"We didn't buy it," Laura whispers. "Mona stole it. We didn't even know she took it until we were outside the store and she gave it to us."

I stay quiet, listening to Laura's breathing on the other end of the line.

"Hey," she says in a loud voice again. "You wanna hang out at our house tomorrow?"

"Yeah, I'll be there." I decide never, ever to miss another adventure with my friends, even if it means going against Mamá's wishes. Unless Papá comes home.

# III

## 19 INEZ

**"Those are the rules."**

"So why are you staying home from school on Friday?" Laura asks as we cross the empty sports field.

We just finished volleyball practice. Laura and I are the only seventh graders on the team. Our eighth-grade teammates like us, but we don't hang out with them because they think we're kids.

"Family stuff." A gust of wind forces us to hold down our skirts. I can't tell Laura that on Friday I'm going to see my dad in jail.

"I figured something was up because you *never* miss school. Remember last year, when they wouldn't give you a certificate for perfect attendance?"

It was fun getting a certificate for perfect attendance at the end of every school year. Bad weather, illness—nothing kept me from attending class. But when I enrolled in my new school, Bowie Elementary, they refused to issue a certificate in my name.

"What was the bullshit excuse they gave you?" Laura asks.

"Can't remember," I say, even though every word is stuck in my brain.

"Inez missed three days of class," the teacher explained when students defended me.

"That's because she was attending another school," a student protested.

"Correct, and those days counted as absences."

"But she attended class every day after she enrolled here!" another student insisted. "That doesn't make sense."

"Those are the rules." The teacher gave me a dirty look. She made me feel like I was trying to get away with something. It was embarrassing. That was the day I stopped caring about certificates for perfect attendance.

"What a bunch of assholes!" Laura rants. "You were in school every day."

"Assholes." I'm learning so many new words from the sisters, I have to repeat them so I don't forget. "So are you going with Mona to Carol's party on Saturday?"

Laura removes a pack of Kools from her pocket as soon as we step off school property. She offers me one.

"No, she's going with Nicky. I can't believe you don't want to go with us."

I take the cigarette and turn my back against the wind to light it. I saw someone do that in a movie. I'm glad when Laura changes the subject.

"Hey, did I tell you Mona told Liz she let Nicky touch her?" Laura asks, raising an eyebrow.

"What do you mean, touch her?"

"You know! She let Nicky touch her titties."

"Why would she do that?"

"She wants him to like her. You know what that makes her?"

Laura and I look at each other without saying a word.

Mamá's told me that if a boy touches me, he'll never marry me.

"You mean like if a boy touches my hand?" I didn't mention holding hands with Petey in the fifth grade and with Johnny last year.

"*Graciosa*, you're funny. I mean if they touch private parts of your body that you only share with your husband."

My mother was talking about sex but you'd never know it. I have so many questions like, how does sex work? Why is it okay to have sex if you're married but it's a bad thing if you're not? Why bother asking? Mamá will never answer.

I'm also beginning to question this whole idea about being a "good" girl. When Petey and I held hands, he asked me to be his girlfriend. When I refused to kiss Johnny, he found another girl.

"Now we know why Mona has a boyfriend," I say.

"Would you let a boy touch you, just to have a boyfriend?" Laura asks.

"No. Would you?"

"What if he's already your boyfriend?"

"Still no, because he'll never marry me."

"Why wouldn't he marry you?" Laura sounds concerned.

"A girl has to be *pure* to get married."

"What about boys? Don't they have to be pure?"

"Boys can't be pure," I tease and toss the cigarette butt to the ground.

"Why?"

"Boys are born messy, dirty as dirt."

We burst out laughing and dash up the stairs of Laura's house.

A slow melody drifts through the door of the sisters' bedroom. When we walk in, Liz is sitting on one of the beds painting her fingernails.

"Hello," she says, dipping a small brush into the bottle of polish.

"Hello." I check out the dresser holding all sorts of makeup. My parents don't let me wear it so it's a treat to see what the sisters are buying.

"Where's Yoli?" Laura asks, brushing her long hair.

"Out with friends." Liz spreads her fingers to admire her work. The platinum-colored nail polish pops out against her brown skin. "Yoli says sophomores can't hang out with little girls."

"What little girls?" I ask, picking up a can of hairspray.

"She's talking about *us*," Liz says. "I swear, sometimes you just don't get it."

"*You're* the one who doesn't get it!" Laura hollers.

We start laughing, but Liz doesn't think we're funny.

"Ha-ha."

"What's the name of this song?" I ask, spraying hairspray on my hair.

"'Sitting on the Dock of the Bay,' by Otis Redding. Do you like it?" Liz asks.

"It's kinda sad."

"That's because you like crap by Donovan or Tommy James and the Shondells."

"You act like you know everything," Laura chides her sister.

"I know something you don't!" Liz taunts. "I know Mona is going all the way with Nicky this summer."

"Who told you?" Laura demands.

"Mona." Liz smiles.

"Why would she tell you that?" Laura asks. "I bet she's lying."

"Why would she lie?"

"Why would she tell you she's going to behave like a whore?"

"Mona loves Nicky," Liz argues.

"Oh, please. It still makes her a whore. Right, Inez?"

"Well, yeah. I mean, if you go all the way."

"What's wrong with you?" Liz sneers at me.

"Nothing's wrong."

Sometimes Liz acts like she's jealous of my friendship with Laura. Maybe it's because we spend time together during volleyball practice. Not my fault Liz hates sports.

"I bet you think Nicky likes you," Liz taunts.

My mouth opens but no words come out.

"Shut up, Liz," Laura scolds. "You don't know what you're talking about."

"Mona doesn't like the way Nicky and Inez are always talking and flirting."

I can't believe what I'm hearing. Nicky and I talk about music, but that doesn't mean I have a crush on him. My voice finally returns.

"Nicky's the one who talks to *me* and I never flirt with him!"

"Yeah, Nicky's the motherfucker," Laura says, showing off a new curse word.

"I wouldn't mess with Mona. She fights like a boy. You better watch out, Inez. "

"Fight? How did we get to fighting?" I can't believe Mona thinks Nicky likes me. She's so much prettier than me. Mona doesn't have my big nose, the one Carlitos teases me about. Nicky's cute but not gorgeous—not enough to get beaten up for. I also remember Mamá said ladies don't fight and women who do are vulgar. "If Mona thinks I'm after Nicky, why doesn't she ask me?"

"Because Mona's chicken," Laura says.

"She is not!" Liz screams.

"People who talk about others behind their back are chicken!" Laura insists.

The girls are still arguing when the needle on the record player lifts and another 45 record drops on the platter. A woman's voice explodes through the speakers.

"Inez, this is the song I told you about." Laura dashes to the middle of the room. "Come on, let's dance the shing-a-ling to Aretha's new record, *RESPECT*!"

"Who's Aretha?"

"The Queen of Soul!" Liz starts dancing and singing.

Mona may want to fight but dancing the shing-a-ling to Aretha is more exciting.

# III

## 20 AMALIA

**All of us visiting loved ones caged like animals...**

MI NIÑA'S OVERNIGHT visits to Juárez stopped some time ago. No more camping in the yard on hot summer nights, sharing stories under the stars until Inez fell asleep. She even skipped the yearly trek through the mountains to collect wild sage for the nativity scene this past Christmas. *Mi niña* still loves me but I know Katalina keeps her from visiting.

The other night, when I found out Inez had been alone with those agents, I wanted so badly to bring her home with me.

"Juana was with her," Amá chided when I shared my grief. But they left her alone! I wanted to scream.

"It is what it is, nothing you can do to fix it," Amá added. She's right, yet I can't help wanting to make things better for the kids.

This afternoon when Emilio and I arrived at the El Paso County Jail, I expected Katalina and the kids to be waiting in line together. Instead, *mis niños* are alone, surrounded by strangers, mostly Negro and Hispanic women chatting with each other while their children run around playing. Eduardo explains that Katalina had to work and he's in charge until she gets here. *Qué desdicha*; the tragedy of condemning children to the consequences of their parents' deeds.

I look around at all the people visiting loved ones who have been branded criminals and are caged like animals. When did Ramón lose our family's values? Some say he was never the same after that drowning incident. I don't believe it.

I can still see Ramón's friends pulling him out of the pond.

"*Lo siento*," the city doctor proclaimed.

We were devastated when the doctor said our boy was gone. With a heavy heart I began funeral arrangements. But Amá held a vigil by Ramón's bedside. She massaged his chest with herbal tonics and lotions, praying through the night.

The next morning Ramón awoke as if nothing had happened. The man of science returned.

"*¡Imposible!*" he declared. "The boy had no pulse and was deprived of oxygen, yet there seems to be no brain damage."

Amá and I fell to our knees. We witnessed a miracle and were not about to question divinity. Until recently, we traveled to Mexico City on an annual pilgrimage to thank *La Virgen de Guadalupe* for Ramón's recovery, crawling on our knees across the courtyard until we reached the entrance to the cathedral.

Today I pray *La Virgen* forgives me for not visiting her this past year. *Madre de Dios*, grant me another miracle! Return my son home. I light another cigarette, dry the tears welling up against my wishes and reach for Emilio's arm.

# III

## 21 KATALINA

**How can everyone be so at ease?**

THE SUN SHINES without warming the cold wind. The fake-fur collar of my wool coat flutters, brushing against my skin. My brow crinkles as I approach the line of people at the El Paso County Jail.

The line starts in the underground garage. I follow it around the corner onto San Antonio Avenue. Amalia, Emilio, and my children stand at the end. I should've asked for the day off but the factory bosses may think I'm taking advantage of this situation.

The memory of yesterday's meeting with Ramón's attorney adds to my anxiety. Ralph Torres wasted no time in making me aware of the problem. He told me how and why Ramón and his friends were arrested.

"Mrs. Ramirez, your telephone is still under surveillance and Ramón's Mustang has been confiscated. Be aware spouses are always suspect in contraband cases."

"*¡Qué tontería!*" The idea of being considered a suspect was nonsense, yet it scared me. What would happen to my children if I went to prison?

"Don't worry," Ralph assured me. "The surveillance cleared you and I'm working on getting rid of the tap on your phone."

It was shocking to learn people had been listening to our phone conversations. Was this the reason Ramón started using public telephones?

"One more thing. There is little I can do for Ramón, unless—"

"Is that because we can't pay for your services?"

Ralph Torres leaned back in his chair, a scowl transforming the nondescript features of his face.

"The quality of my service does not depend on reimbursement. I doubt you can afford my private fee unless Ramón left assets you haven't mentioned. If that's the case, I advise you to be careful, Mrs. Ramirez."

"You must think we're all criminals!" His words annoyed me, but his warning made me think. I agreed to help.

"*Muy bien*," Ralph said, smiling. "Ramón must consider providing the names of his bosses, the people running this operation. Have you met them?"

My voice cracked. "I barely know the men you mentioned."

"Any information Ramón provides will be helpful."

Alejandro's phone call came to mind. His tone when he mentioned my family's safety—it sounded more threatening than ever. "Isn't that dangerous?" I asked.

"Your husband put your family in danger. Ramón has decided not to cooperate with the authorities. You need to convince him otherwise."

Keep quiet, is what Alejandro meant when he said Ramón and I knew what to do.

One thing becomes clear as I approach my children in line

to visit their father in jail. I don't have the strength or means to save our kids *and* Ramón. If this is a matter of choice, I've made it. Our children will survive this ordeal.

Eduardo waves to me. People have already joined the line behind the kids.

"Patricia decided to stay home," Emilio tells me when I arrive. I'm pleased. Fewer people means more time for Ramón and me.

At exactly three o'clock, the line starts moving towards the entrance. When we reach the door, a policeman stands repeating an announcement: "All personal items will be inspected. Packages left for inmates will be delivered at the discretion of this institution. We reserve the right to refuse visitations. Visiting hours end promptly at five o'clock."

Ralph Torres gave me a list of items to bring Ramón.

"Will they confiscate the things we brought?" I ask Eduardo.

"Calm down, *cuñada*," Emilio cautions.

How can everyone be so at ease? Emilio and the children keep looking around as if they want to remember every detail to recount at a later date. Even Amalia, whom I expected to panic, wears her old air of calm authority as we approach the inspection area.

Bare bulbs hanging from the ceiling cast dark shadows, adding a sinister feeling to the noisy and chilly building. Security guards stand behind wooden tables searching through the personal property of every visitor. Someone takes my purse while another officer takes the paper bag Carlitos is holding.

"Name of the inmate you're visiting," a guard asks, looking down at a clipboard.

Eduardo responds: "Ramón Ramirez."

I hope the *Americano* doesn't think my boy is interfering. My son takes the responsibility of assisting me very seriously.

Another agent dumps out the paper bag. Several pairs of underwear and socks land on the counter next to a carton of cigarettes. It's humiliating to see the public display of my husband's private clothing.

Next to the cigarettes is a notepad and box of pencils I don't remember packing. The children must have brought the items for their father. The agent returns everything to the paper bag, writes 5D on the side, and places it with other bundles for inmates. At the end of the table, another guard is searching Inez's handbag.

*Temor y pesar*; fear grips my being, regret rips my soul. Why can't children arrive with instructions and parents with warnings?

# |||

## 22 INEZ

**I'm not ashamed—I love my dad!**

IF ONLY I could pop into a bottle like the genie on TV. Or twitch my nose and fix everything like Samantha on *Bewitched*—anything so I don't have to tell Papá I put him in prison.

The officer who took my purse removes a pack of tissues and Beechnut gum from inside. No need to ask Mamá if I can share this adventure with Laura and Liz. Too bad. There's so much to tell. The officer returns the items to my bag and hands it back to me.

"Okay, little lady, you may join your family." He smiles and gestures to an elevator. "You're all set to go up."

No one talks in the crowded elevator that takes forever to climb the building. As soon as the elevator door opens on the fifth floor, people dash out and scatter through the halls. This place looks like a hospital with white walls and polished floors. I can even smell Pine-Sol disinfectant. Where are the steel bars like the jails on *Gunsmoke*?

Eduardo leads us down a hall lined with steel doors. There

are no doorknobs but each door has a little window and a small box underneath it.

An inmate smiles at me as I pass his door. I feel frightened—no, embarrassed.... I'm not sure. When Eduardo stops to ask a guard for directions, I hang back and stroke my marble charm. Marshal Dillon of *Gunsmoke* appears beside me.

"What's the matter, little lady?"

"I'm confused," I say.

"Could it be you're embarrassed by your family's dilemma?"

"What does that mean?"

"Are you ashamed to see your father in jail?"

"I'm not ashamed of Papá. I love my dad!"

"Of course you do, but sometimes people we love do things that upset us."

"That's it!" Eduardo points to a door a few feet away. "Papá is in 5D."

My heart jumps, and Marshal Dillon disappears into thin air. A woman crouches by the door Eduardo pointed to. Turns out the little box is an intercom. A small boy hides behind the woman's skirt. She pauses to make sure he's all right.

"I thought we'd be sitting at a table," Mamá says. She glances at her watch.

A few minutes pass before the woman picks up the little boy. The inmate on the other side suddenly stands up. His body blocks the window as I try to get a glimpse of Papá.

"Say goodbye to your brother, *mi'jo*," the woman says. She kisses her fingers and presses them against the glass.

"Bye, Chuy!" The little boy waves his baby hand.

The woman turns and smiles at Mamá. "Federal prisons

have tables and chairs," she says before leading the little boy away.

I wish I could follow them out of this building where I put my dad.

# III

## 23 RAMÓN

**Wounds inflicted by loved ones
sometimes don't heal at all.**

THE LAST THING a man wants is to have his family witness his most vulnerable moment. My throat chokes up with raw emotion.

I expected my mother's tears, and sure enough I see Mamá crying through the prison cell window. Next to her is Katalina, looking confused but composed as always. I summon the courage to smile at my children.

Nothing prepared me for the discerning looks on their faces. The kids stare at me as if they've solved a puzzle that had been troubling them and in the process matured without aging, innocence vanished.

Katalina steps forward. I switch on the intercom.

"*¿Cómo estas?*" I ask.

Katalina shrugs.

"Did you bring cigarettes?"

She nods.

"*Gracias,*" I whisper.

"Ralph Torres says you need to cooperate with the authorities." Katalina's voice chirps through the intercom.

"*¡Claro que no!*" I snap. "You don't understand the consequences."

"*¿Consecuencia?*" Katalina's voice rises. "Our family is *living* the consequences." She looks at the floor before continuing. "I can't post your bail without money."

I lower my voice to a whisper. "Katalina, you need to liquidate the—"

"Emilio is already looking into it."

"*Ya vez*, my brother will work things out, don't worry."

"I have a right to be upset—"

"You have a right but we're not going to resolve this matter here. Let me speak with the rest of the family while you calm down." It annoys me that Katalina insists on discussing things we can't fix.

My mother approaches the door in tears. I can't remember the last time she held me, yet I feel the warmth of her body.

"*¡Mi'jo!*" Mamá wails without activating the intercom.

"Push the button, *señora!*" Katalina hollers.

I clutch the doorframe while Carlitos helps his grandmother.

"*Tus abuelitos…*" Mamá sobs into the intercom. "Your grandparents and I pray for your return home!"

It's hopeless; I have no words to comfort my mother. She starts wailing again. Emilio removes her from the door. He returns a few seconds later.

"Don't worry, *hermano*," he assures me. "I'll sell the business and get you out of here."

"I know I can count on you."

Katalina doubts Emilio has our best interests at heart. It's because I can't explain my little brother's habit of rummaging through our belongings. The practice started when we were teens. Emilio took the most absurd things from me—handkerchiefs, socks—which he tossed when he thought no one was looking. How can you hold such silly behavior against your brother? And now I have no choice but to trust that Emilio will look after my family while I'm locked up in here.

Eduardo follows his uncle to the door.

"I'll make sure our family is safe," Eduardo says.

"I know you will." My heart breaks but I smile as my boy walks away.

Responsibility for a parent is not the legacy I intended for my son. I felt the burden of that obligation with Mamá. She even treated me like the head of the family, until my opinions interfered with her goals, at which point she exerted her power, dismissing my judgment and blaming my frustration on youthful rebellion.

Wounds inflicted by loved ones sometimes don't heal at all. I learned that lesson from my son Carlitos, the most sensitive of our children.

I was still with the Department of Sanitation when a schedule change had me working our own family's neighborhood. I was driving the truck but jumped out to help my colleagues. Carlitos and a group of children approached as I emptied the last trash bin. He stared right at me, then ran across the street without acknowledging me.

My son's snub crushed me. The memory still hurts, but I smile at the boy who once broke my heart as he approaches the door of my cell.

"I brought paper and pencils so you can write to us, okay?" Carlitos hollers through the intercom.

"You bet I'll write," I say. How can one convince a child that the opinions of others don't matter, when they do?

"*Basta, Carlitos,*" Katalina urges. "It's time to let your sister talk to your father."

Carlitos waves goodbye. Inez hesitates, which is not like her.

My daughter displayed her feisty personality soon after her birth. I recall passing by her cradle where she lay looking around with a puckered brow, as if trying to figure out where in the world she had landed.

At the moment, Inez stares at me as if I'm injured and there is nothing she can do to help.

"*Ándale, Inez,*" Katalina says. "Hurry up. We don't have all day."

My wife frets, but she's a good mother. Our kids look to her for everything. Sometimes I wonder if I'm even needed by my family. One thing I know for sure. My world already feels lonely without them.

# III

## 24 INEZ

**Being careful means, be careful around boys.**

THE ROLLER COASTER ride at Western Playland makes my stomach queasy when I go up and down on its peaks and valleys. I have that same feeling approaching the door to talk to my father. Papá smiles and bends toward the intercom.

"*Hola, mi'ja,* how are you?" Papá's voice sounds fuzzy and tinny.

"I'm fine." I lower my gaze. Adults have special powers; they can look into your eyes and tell you're lying.

"How are you doing in school?"

Papá's prompting perks me up. I look right into his eyes.

"I got four As, two Bs, and won two ribbons in volleyball."

"Well, maybe you can work on changing those Bs to As."

"Yes, sir."

"Be careful out there," Papá warns.

Being careful means, be careful around boys.

"Yes, sir."

"Remember, no boyfriends until you're thirty."

I smile at my dad.

"Say goodbye, Inez," Mamá nags.

"Inez, take care of your mama." Papá smiles.

I nod and stare at the floor, my throat choking with words stuck inside.

*"Por favor, Inez,"* Mamá demands. "Please, I need to speak with your father."

My mother's pestering pisses me off. There's so much I need to tell Papá.

I want him to know how frightening it was having FBI agents searching our home. How I hate to see Mamá and Abuelita crying. How I don't understand what he's done but how afraid I am that he's never coming home. Most of all, I want to tell him I love him and I'm sorry for putting him in jail. I want to say that and more, but instead I turn away, pushing Mamá aside.

No goodbye, no "Papá, I love you." I just want to go home and be alone.

# III

## 25 INEZ

**There are no paintings or statues in Mamá's church.**

RELIGION IS RIGHT up there on my list of "strange." When I was little, Abuelita took me to Catholic cathedrals filled with beautiful paintings and elegant statues. Every year we traveled to the church of *La Virgen de Guadalupe* in Mexico City. Abuelita and Tía Patricia crawled on their knees across the plaza until they reached the entrance to the cathedral.

I loved Los Matachines, the dancers dressed as Indians who perform in front of the church to the steady beat of their drums. The fancy beading and plumage of their costumes were so different from the dark robes of *el padre santo* and the nuns.

There are no paintings or statues in Mamá's church. No crosses on the wall, no votive candles lit for saints, and no smell of incense during Mass.

"Evangelicals don't believe in saints," Mamá explained. "And God's image cannot be replicated."

Yeah, okay! I think of Mona with her Twiggy haircut and stolen makeup. What would she say about Mamá's religion which forbids women to wear makeup and cut their hair? My mother and Tía Chayo wear lipstick outside of church. They also have short hair which they cover with lace *mantillas*.

Mamá and Tía Chayo should wear *rebozos* like most of the other women. The dark cotton of the shawls would hide their haircuts. Everyone can see through the lace, which is probably why the sisters prefer the back row of the church.

That's where we sit this Sunday morning. Mamá nudges me when I start swinging my legs back and forth under the pew. I glare back, still pissed off at her for not allowing me more time with Papá. I'm also annoyed Mamá bought my brothers' lame excuses for not coming to church.

"I have to finish a school project," Eduardo told her. "Visiting Papá on Friday set me back a bit."

"If Eduardo isn't going to Juárez, I'm not going either," Carlitos declared.

"Me neither," I said.

"Well, someone's going with me, and I pick you as my escort, Inez."

The boys chuckled. I didn't think it was funny.

Mamá ignores my dirty look and whispers to Tía Chayo. They gesture toward their brother Tío Enrique. He and his family sit in the front row with my grandparents.

Abuelita Febronia adjusts the *rebozo* covering her head and shoulders. Abuelito Felipe fiddles with his cowboy hat while a young minister preaches from the pulpit. The thin, worn fabric of the minister's suit makes me shiver. The flames of the kerosene heater beside him blaze through the glass but do nothing to heat the frosty chill.

"*Vamos a orar,*" the minister instructs. "Let us pray for two families who are in need of our Lord's guidance, *la familia Lira y la familia Ramirez.* After our prayer we will praise our Lord with a hymn."

Everyone stands. I turn to Mamá who looks surprised to hear the minister mention our name. After the prayer, a young man strikes the keys of an upright piano. This is my favorite part of the service, until someone sings off-key.

"Why do people sing if they don't have good voices?" I once complained.

"*Himnos* praise God and *He* isn't picky about the way you sing," Mamá explained.

He should be, I think, as everyone around me starts praising God with hymns.

# III

## 26 KATALINA

**Today I need my church to help light my way.**

YOUTHFUL TEMPTATIONS CLASHED with the strict doctrine of my parents' faith when I was fourteen. What young girl can resist the latest fashions, powdering her face and attending monthly dances? Papá protested: "I won't have you mocking our faith, Katalina!" Perhaps he was tired of people like Amalia criticizing his religion.

"Evangelicals are heathens!" my mother-in-law is fond of saying.

Amalia seems to have a problem only with *my* religion. I know for a fact Don Sabino has never stepped foot in a church in his life.

Taunts never kept me away. I've always been comforted by my religion, and attend services whenever I can. Today, I need my church to help light my way.

The hymns end, and the minister makes his way to the exit. He stands shaking hands with male parishioners and blessing women as we leave.

Outside, the sunlight warms my face. Inez, Chayo, and I stand aside to wait for our parents. My brother Enrique and his family arrive first. He strokes Inez's head. She smiles, greets the family, and walks off with her cousins.

Chayo's husband Lázaro joins us. He's Catholic like Ramón. They often waited together while we attended church service. "How's Ramón?" Lázaro asks.

Before I can answer, Papá and Mamá arrive with the minister. Papá puts on his cowboy hat. Mamá adjusts her *rebozo*. I thank the minister for the prayer.

"The congregation will continue to pray for your family, Katalina," he says.

His words are comforting although I'm embarrassed that the entire congregation is aware of my family's predicament.

I ask the minister about Juana, our housekeeper. His wife originally recommended her for the job.

The minister smiles. "God protects the innocent. Juana's safe. She was deported but saved her documents by hiding them in her Bible. The visa was issued for leisure, not employment. Juana was afraid the FBI agents would confiscate it, so she told them she had no papers."

Everyone chuckles; I blush. "Please offer her my apologies."

The minister strokes my arm. "I will give Juana your regards, no apologies. God be with you."

After the minister leaves, Mamá breaks the silence. "Katalina, we found out about Ramón on Wednesday. I should've gone to see you, but we thought you needed privacy. I'm sorry. How are you?"

Papá lowers his head.

"*Estoy bien*," I mutter, assuring them all is well. I shy away from my mother's touch, afraid I'll fall apart if she tries to comfort me.

III

My parents' faith affects every aspect of their life. Their modest home reflects the belief that material goods promote pride and arrogance. This house on the outskirts of Juárez is a smaller version of the one Papá built back in their hometown of San Agustin. It has the same whitewashed adobe walls and homemade doors and windows. The house sits on a ridge, overlooking the neighborhood.

Papá leads us through the small courtyard paved by parched soil imbedded with gravel. We step into a large room with cement floors. The kids plop down onto two twin beds while the adults settle down at a table in the corner.

Enrique starts a fire in the wood stove. Mamá removes her husband's coat and takes his Bible. Mamá was fifteen and Papá was twenty when they met. They married the following year. Mamá has catered to his whims and wishes ever since.

"Let me make some *cafecito*," Mamá says. Her dimples light up her smile as she scurries off to the kitchen.

"How's Ramón?" Papá asks.

"Katalina, tell Papá the amount of Ramón's bail," Chayo coaxes.

"No need, Katalina," he says, then turns to my sister. "*Por favor*, why must you be so childish!" It always surprises me to hear our father scolding her.

Papá always favored Chayo and Enrique. I was convinced he used up all his love on them and had none left for the rest of us kids. How else could a little girl justify a father's indifference? Sometimes it's hard to hide my resentment about Papá's decisions. Today, I want my father to feel my pain with me.

"I don't mind sharing the information. Ramón's bail is five thousand U.S. dollars."

"*¡Dios mío!*" Enrique's wife exclaims.

Mamá returns from the kitchen with a pot of steaming coffee and sets it down on the table.

"Where will you get so much money?" asks Chayo's husband, Lázaro.

"Emilio is selling our business—"

"*¿La cantina?* According to Emilio, it's making money. Why would you sell it?"

"You've spoken with Emilio?"

"He came into my workplace. A guy at the garage is selling a truck. Emilio is interested in purchasing it."

My stomach churns with misgivings.

"What will you do until you sell the business?" Enrique asks.

"Ramón has been assigned an attorney free of charge."

"*¿Gratis?*" Enrique asks. "You don't have to pay for the service?"

Papá's brow creases. His frown deepens with every word of my explanation about Ramón's attorney. I sense Papá is having a hard time believing *los Americanos* possess the kind of generosity I'm describing. It contradicts what his grandfather Amador told him, stories my father shared with us kids.

"*Los Americanos* arrived in *Tejas* to confiscate Mexican property and killed anyone who got in their way." Our father echoed our great-grandfather's conviction: "*Pa' mi*, Texas will always be Mexican territory."

A lot of family members agree. We have ancestors who refused to leave their homes when Mexico lost its territories to the United States in the 1800s. They had to accept the terms of the Hidalgo Treaty which made them American citizens.

Papá can recount every detail about our ancestors but is vague about our immediate family history. Mamá does her best to fill in the gaps. According to her story, Papá's brother moved to *Tejas* as a teenager and lived with relatives who had been born in Texas. Papá refused to join him until 1925, when the economic devastation of the Mexican Revolution forced hundreds of Mexicans to flee across the Rio Grande into *los Estados Unidos*. Mamá and the older children followed a year later.

My family lived in Texas for more than a decade before the Immigration Service paid a visit. Mamá described how a tall white man with a red, suntanned face translated the information from a piece of paper: "Mr. Fuentes, we received this here order from Washington, D.C., asking that we verify the legal status of all our residents. I know your family has been blessed with several children since your arrival. They, of course, are American citizens by virtue of their birth. However, anyone who arrived from Mexico must file paperwork at our office. Failure to comply leaves us no choice but to deport you and your family. You have thirty days."

Mamá says they had no idea that from time to time the United States government gathered Mexicans and shipped them back to Mexico, even if they had been born in America. They felt lucky to get a warning.

"*Los Estados Unidos* imposes laws to keep Mexicans out until *los güeros* need cheap labor," my father supposedly told my mother. "I won't ask permission to live in *any* country."

The stock market crash of 1929 had plunged the United States into the Great Depression, and a severe drought destroyed the agricultural heartland of America. Mexican labor was unwanted.

Papá had kept up with the presidential campaign of Lázaro Cárdenas in Mexico. The Mexican candidate promised to divide the large parcels of land owned by a small group of landowners and several foreign companies. Papá reasoned that if Cárdenas won, laborers like him would be granted an opportunity to own the land they worked.

One month after receiving the notice from the United States government, Papá packed up the family. A week later we stepped off the train in San Agustin, Mexico. I'm told the older children carried boxes and luggage. I arrived as a toddler tugging at Mamá's skirt while Chayo slept in a *rebozo* strapped to our mother's back.

Papá received a parcel of land from the Mexican government and never visited the United States again, though eventually our parents followed us to *la frontera* and settled in Juárez.

Some of his children have yet to forgive him for leaving the United States. For those born in America, his decision to return to Mexico made us strangers in our place of birth.

I enjoyed growing up in Mexico and don't fault my parents for leaving the United States. My resentment stems from the decision Papá made later in life, the harshest: turning his back on me.

*Una eternidad*: Papá must understand some mistakes are everlasting.

# III

## 27 INEZ

**For one moment,
he made me hate my dad.**

SOMETIMES KIDS KEEP parts of their home lives to themselves. Not secrets someone told them not to tell, just things in life we have a hard time understanding. I couldn't talk to Laura about my dad, but she knew.

One day, I stopped to pick up the sisters on the way to school. I knocked on the door but no one heard me. The last time I did that Mrs. Vargas gave me permission to come in if the door was open. That's what I did that morning, walked into the kitchen while they hung out in the bedroom. That's when I overheard the sisters and their mother talking.

"Inez's father was arrested for selling pot," Yoli was telling the girls.

"Why would anyone get arrested for selling a pot?" Liz scoffed.

"It's not *a* pot, you idiot," Yoli explained. "It's *pot*, like marijuana pot. All the rock bands and freaks in California are smoking it to get high. Inez's father is cool!"

"There's nothing *cool* about getting arrested," their mother added. "And how is it you know so much about pot, Yolanda?"

"I read about it in the paper, Ma!"

"You better be only reading about it. And don't mention this to Inez, unless she brings it up. It's not polite to throw people's dirty laundry in their face."

I slipped out of the sisters' house before they saw me, then knocked hard until they heard me.

Laura never mentioned the conversation, just like I kept my visit to the jailhouse to myself. I waited two days before asking Laura what the word freak means. It didn't make sense they would be talking about a circus freak or some other oddity.

"Yoli says a freak is a super cool guy but it also means you're worried or scared, like when you freak or you're freaking out."

"Freaking out. Cool!" I said. We laughed and I tried not to think about my father.

It's been over a month since I've seen Papá. I miss him, but Mamá says we can't take every Friday off from school to visit him.

This morning, Lalo is the first person to greet me when Laura and I walk into the classroom.

"Does your mother know you wear makeup?" he asks, looking straight at me.

Where is Mrs. Rogers when you need her?

"Does your mother know you're a faggot?" Laura taunts my neighbor.

The students are still chuckling when Mrs. Rogers arrives.

"Settle down, class! Lalo, please collect the homework assignment. I need to see Principal Brady." Our teacher walks off to the principal's office.

Lalo gets up from his desk and starts collecting papers.

"Do you have your homework?" he asks.

"No, I forgot it," I mutter.

"Again."

"Hey, what's it to you, creep?" Laura scolds.

"I wasn't talking to you!" Lalo snaps, "so mind your business."

"Mind your business," Laura whines, mocking Lalo. "You are such an asshole."

"Why don't you shut your filthy mouth?" he hisses.

"And why don't you shut up, motherfucker!" I blurt out.

Lalo's eyes and mouth pop open. He looks like he's freaking out, but he recovers and smiles.

"Why don't you go smoke some of that marijuana your dad's been selling around town?"

Lalo's words stop my world. Pounding inside my head, their sound pins me to the ground. I want to run but can't move. Without warning tears gush down my cheeks. I can't stop them.

Ricardo rushes into the classroom as I try to wipe my face clean.

"What happened?" he asks.

"Lalo made her cry," Laura volunteers. "He said something about her father."

Ricardo turns to Lalo. "What's wrong with you?"

"She—she called me—a motherfucker." Lalo sounds scared.

"So you made her cry?" Ricardo walks over and kicks Lalo's chair. "You're a jerk. You better watch yourself!"

I want Ricardo to hurt Lalo, because for one moment he made me hate my dad.

Tears well up again. This time I escape to the hallway.

I stand staring straight ahead, willing myself to stop crying. That's when I see Mona watching me.

She's walking from the other end of the hallway. If she wants to fight I'm ready to get vulgar. Out of nowhere Nicky steps in front of me.

"Are you all right?" He squints with concern.

I nod, wiping my eyes.

"What's the matter, your dad spank you for going out?" Mona chuckles.

Nicky nudges her.

"Hey!" Mona hollers.

I ignore them and make my way toward the bathroom. Once inside, the tears return. The tile walls echo with my sobbing. I rub my marble charm, but no one comes to my rescue. The gold chain cuts my skin when I yank it from my neck.

"I *hate* you!" I slam the round sphere against the wall. The marble charm shatters and I stop sobbing.

Never, ever again will anyone see me cry.

# III

## 28 KATALINA

**Cómo es posible, Ramón leaving me to
deal with such idiots?**

THE EIGHTH DAY of December 1659, Franciscan brother
Fray García de San Francisco laid the foundation for La Misión de Nuestra Señora de Guadalupe de los Mansos del Paso
del Norte. The unassuming structure built by Manso Indians
under the direction of Fray Garcia was completed on January
15, 1668, in what is now downtown Juárez.

This historical fact is printed on a plaque that I read on
the day of Inez's christening. The Catholic ceremony—which
I opposed—took place at La Misión.

"*Mi niña* will not grow up a heathen," Amalia insisted. She
repeated her belief that Evangelicals are not Christians.

On this February day in 1967, Emilio and I sit on a bench
in the plaza. Facing us is the classical façade of a more recent
addition, La Catedral de Nuestra Señora de Guadalupe de
Ciudad Juárez. The twin steeples of this church, built in 1957,
overshadow the modest Misión next door. The clock of the
*catedral* strikes noon.

*Mediodía* is the time Alejandro instructed me to meet him.
He waited exactly one month after Ramón's arrest to contact

me again, calling two nights ago at one a.m., piercing another nightmare of disturbing images.

"Hello?" I whispered.

"Mrs. Ramirez, I'm calling on behalf of a friend."

I recognized Alejandro's voice before asking what he wanted.

"Your friend wants to meet across the street from *La Virgen de Guadalupe* cathedral in Juárez. Sunday at twelve noon."

When I told the family about Alejandro's call, Emilio immediately decided to join me at the meeting. "You shouldn't be alone with such a dangerous man." For once, Amalia and I agreed.

The plaza is teeming with people and soon church bells start ringing, gathering the faithful to the twelve o'clock mass. I decide to have a cigarette while we wait for Alejandro. I reach inside my purse as my gaze searches the crowd. I feel the pack of Lucky Strikes but leave it because Alejandro just appeared.

*"Aquí viene,"* I announce his arrival to Emilio.

Alejandro's dark sunglasses stand out in the crowd. His body casts a shadow when he stops in front of me. He smiles, offering me a small white box tied with string. I refuse it. Alejandro insists, thrusting the box at me. He removes a cigar from his pocket.

"How is your husband?" he asks.

*"Bien,* considering he's in prison." I place the box between Emilio and me. Alejandro isn't responsible for Ramón's decisions, but I still resent his existence.

"Sometimes you gamble and lose, but you married a smart man," Alejandro says.

"How may we help you?" Emilio asks.

"You're not capable of helping anyone but yourself, Emilio." Alejandro gestures to the bench. I move the box, and he sits between Emilio and me. "I hear someone is embezzling money from Ramón's business."

My lips part without speaking.

Alejandro smiles when he notices my surprise.

"I'm not here to discuss your business, Katalina. I do want to offer some advice." He pauses to light the cigar. "Don't be pressured into making bad decisions. Your family will get hurt if your husband assists the authorities. You're a sensible woman and Ramón is doing the right thing by keeping quiet." Alejandro points to the box. "It's a gift for your smart husband."

After struggling with the string, I finally lift the cover and stare at the box filled with pastries.

"What is this?" I groan.

"Lift the wax paper underneath," Alejandro instructs.

My hand trembles when I see hundred dollar bills lining the bottom of the box.

"We hope it helps with your husband's legal fees."

"*Gracias*, but we don't need it." I close the box.

"Of course we need it!" Emilio says, turning his gaze from the box to me.

*Have you no pride taking money from a criminal?* I want to scream.

"Of course you need it!" Alejandro mocks Emilio and chuckles before continuing. "There's more," he says, pointing at the box. "If Ramón continues to—"

"That's not necessary," I interrupt. The last thing I want is Alejandro in my life. The man is a fugitive who threatened my family!

"I don't want to have to contact you either, Katalina, so

remember what I said about making sensible decisions. *Buena suerte.*" Alejandro stands up and leaves.

He disappears into the crowd. Emilio gestures toward the box.

"We could use some money to make repairs to the business. It'd be easier to sell."

"Who's embezzling money from *la cantina*?" I recall Lázaro's remark about Emilio stopping by his workplace to look into the sale of a truck.

"*No sé,*" Emilio snaps. "I've no idea what Alejandro is talking about." He lights a cigarette, then reveals someone is interested in taking over the cantina. "It'll take time."

My temples throb. I'm in no mood to discuss the tavern, but Alejandro's remark keeps needling me. Emilio gets up. I follow him.

"*¿Cómo es posible?*" I mumble. "How could Ramón leave me to deal with such idiots?"

Emilio turns to look at me. I'm not sure, but he may have heard my comment. I hope he did, even if it brings Amalia's wrath on me.

# ||| 

## 29 INEZ

**I freak because my baby-doll dress doesn't have a waistline.**

LAURA'S PISSED OFF. Mrs. Rogers threatened to flunk her if she doesn't start handing in her homework. She's also convinced her mom doesn't care about her school grades.

"As long as I pass, it doesn't matter what grades I get."

"You can't pass if you don't hand in your homework and get good grades," I say.

"They passed me last year, and they'll do it again."

"That doesn't make sense."

"It doesn't have to, that's the way it works. No one cares."

Papá always cared. I had to explain the difference between As and Bs to Mamá, but she seems interested in my schoolwork. I don't believe Laura's mother doesn't care.

After school Laura and I meet up with the girls, who are already waiting in the courtyard. Mona looks me over.

"Where have you been?" Laura asks her. "Haven't seen you in a while."

Mona ignores Laura and turns to me.

"Hey, I like your dress," she says. "All the hippie chicks in California are wearing that style. Can I borrow it some time?"

"Inez's dress looks like a tent," Liz remarks.

"It's a baby-doll dress, you moron."

Mona's comment makes us laugh. Liz frowns, her face turns red, then she tries to joke about it.

"So Inez is a baby?" Liz asks laughing.

Mona chuckles. The rest of us stare at Liz without reacting.

"Hey, you guys, Mona wants to show us a cool trick after school. Right, Mona?" Liz smiles at us.

"If you want."

"We have a meeting with Coach Vasquez," Laura says.

"It won't take long," I explain.

"Yeah, okay." Mona smiles at someone standing behind us. "We'll be at the Rexall Drug Store if you want to meet up."

When Laura and I turn to leave, Nicky stands a few feet away. He smiles at me. For the first time ever, I'm glad Mona's watching.

III

THE MEETING WITH Coach Vasquez turns out to be a pep rally for the team.

"We have a good chance of bringing home big trophies this year," she says. "I know your hard work is going to pay off. And I want to thank you eighth graders for supporting and encouraging your seventh-grade teammates."

After our meeting, Laura and I head to the Five Points neighborhood. A poster at the Pershing Movie Theatre advertises *Casino Royale*. The picture shows a woman sprawled on the floor with her back to us. Her entire body is painted with weird, brightly colored designs.

"That woman is naked and she's holding two guns." Laura says.

I've seen women with guns before. Abuelita has pictures of Amá and other women holding rifles but they didn't look like Playboy bunnies. Those women were cloaked in Mexican *rebozos*. In one picture Amá was dressed as a man with belts of bullets criss-crossing her chest. My great-grandmother and the women were *soldaderas*, recruited during the Mexican Revolution.

"Cool," I mutter, staring at the movie poster.

"Sexy," Laura adds.

We giggle.

"Come on, let's go."

We jaywalk across the street and head to the Rexall Drugstore. The salesclerk scowls as we walk through the door.

We find the girls in the diner, sitting on shiny chrome stools with blue upholstery that matches the Formica counter. A waitress flips burgers on the grill. The man sitting next to Mona gets up, places a tip on the counter, and walks away. Mona puts the money in her pocket. Liz giggles, the rest of the group sits quietly with conniving grins. I wonder if anyone else feels bad about the waitress not getting her tip.

"Are you guys eating?" I ask.

"No." Mona twirls on the stool. "We're finished." She stands up.

"Inez and I want to get something to drink," Laura insists.

"No one's stopping you, but we're heading to Sears."

The waitress approaches the counter with burgers for the older couple sitting next to Liz.

"Are you girls finished?" the waitress asks.

"Yes, ma'am," Mona responds.

"That'll be ten cents for each soda."

The girls place their money on the counter.

"This is for you." Mona hands the waitress the tip from the previous customer.

"Now, aren't you sweet? Thank you, honey."

I can tell by the look on the faces of the other girls Mona's behavior baffles them. I think she's creepy but there's something cool about fooling people.

"So what's up?" Laura asks her sister as we follow Mona to the parking lot.

"Mona wants to show us how to take stockings." Liz sounds excited.

"*Take?*" I ask. "You mean *steal?*"

"Have you done this before?" Laura asks Liz.

"No, but I'd like to get a pair of fishnet stockings."

"What happens if we get caught?" I ask.

"Only idiots get caught," Mona snaps, "but don't do it if you're chicken."

"I'm not chicken!" Now I'm determined to steal something.

"Then listen up. When we get to the hosiery department, spread out, don't huddle. Pick out the stockings you want and stuff them in the waistline of your skirt. Press down so the package doesn't stick out. Walk, don't run out of the store."

I freak because my baby-doll dress doesn't have a waistline.

Mona leads us past the shiny white appliances lining the store entrance. We continue toward the hosiery department. Two clerks are busy helping customers. We wander through the aisles. A clerk startles me when she sneaks up behind me.

"May I help you, young lady?"

"No, thank you, I'm just looking." My legs feel like rubber.

Suddenly Mona rushes by. We follow her. I grab a pair of socks on the way out. When we get outside, Mona isn't around.

"We were right behind her. Where'd she disappear to?" Liz asks.

"Let's head back to the Rexall parking lot," I say. The stolen merchandise is making my hands shake.

We find Mona crouching between two cars in the parking lot. She pulls two packages from her waistline.

"I got these!" I say, showing off the socks.

Everyone giggles except Mona.

"I told you any moron could do it. It's as easy as stealing boyfriends. Let's go to Woolworth's."

"Who's stealing boyfriends?" Liz asks.

"Bitches who can't get their own." Mona glares at me.

"Some bitches have taste!" I counter.

Mona's eyes widen. She moves toward me but Laura steps in.

"Stop it, you two!" she screams. "You just pulled off a heist, and now they'll bust you for fighting!"

Laura sounds like a gangster, and everyone laughs—except Mona. She's still glaring at me.

"I have to leave." I walk off.

"Wait up, I'll go with you." Laura follows me.

"Ah, come on," Liz whines. "I don't wanna go home yet."

"So stay, unless you're afraid of walking home in the dark," Laura teases.

"You're a jerk!" Liz hollers at her sister, then turns to Mona. "See you later."

"Go home, little girls, before mommy spanks you!" Mona taunts.

Mamá says it's not nice to make your friends choose sides, but I wish Liz and Laura weren't friendly with Mona. She's the kind of girl you can't trust.

# 30 INEZ

**El Ranchito**

I NEVER WROTE ESSAYS about my summer vacations because mine were always spent with Abuelita visiting relatives in the Mexican village of San Agustin. It's different from hanging out with Mickey and Minnie at Disneyland. Abuelita and Tía Patricia were the only adults on our trips. At first my brothers Eduardo and Carlitos were part of the group of kids that included our cousins Jose and Luzita and me. Last year my brothers decided to stop going and stayed in El Paso with our parents.

Our vacations started with a scramble to find seats for the eight-hour train ride from Juárez to Torreón. Reservations and air-conditioning didn't exist in second class. Overhead racks filled up quickly with bags, boxes, even cages containing live chickens.

Once the train got underway, another battle began for a window seat. I always beat out Jose and Luzita because they're younger than me. After we settled in our seats, white puffy clouds entertained me with shifting images outside the window.

The blue sky stretched over the sand dunes of Samalayuca, one of many *ranchitos* marking the trail. As soon as the train pulled away, each station and its tiny village disappeared.

Food vendors jumped on the train every time it stopped to board passengers. Men, women, even children dashed down the aisles announcing the goodies they carried in buckets and food baskets: "*¡Enchiladas! ¡Gorditas! ¡Cafe con leche!*"

Abuelita bought only drinks from the vendors. "Why pay for something you can make yourself?" she grumbled, unpacking our lunch.

The other thing she spent money on was the taxicab she hired at the Torreón train station. Abuelita liked to make an entrance to her village. Arriving by cab in San Agustin was a big deal because there were more horses than cars on the streets.

As soon as our cab left the highway and entered the village, people gawked from doors and windows. Children ran alongside the car for a peek at the visitors, their small bodies disappearing in the dust left behind by the wheels.

I loved *el ranchito*: the adobe homes, the horses, chickens, cows, and pigs, the irrigation ditches we swam in. Once a month, an old truck with a speaker strapped to its roof drove through the streets announcing the town dance: "*¡Vengan a bailar!*" San Agustin also had a makeshift movie theatre where films were projected against the white wall of a building.

There were only two things I didn't like about San Agustin. One was the teasing I got for being a *pocha*: a mixed-up Mexican who speaks English better than Spanish. The other was not having toilets. Most homes didn't even have outhouses. People had to squat behind a bush on the outskirts of the village. I thought it was funny until I had to hunker down to do my business. How embarrassing when someone sees you!

I've decided not to visit *el ranchito* this year. I'm having too much fun with my friends in El Paso. No one knows it yet, so when we visit Abuelita in Juárez, I freak when Abuelita asks me about it.

"Inez, are you coming with us to *el ranchito* when school lets out this summer?"

I gulp. I don't want to hurt Abuelita's feelings.

"No, Inez is staying home this year," Mamá says. "I need her help with household chores."

I know what's coming next: drama between Mamá and Abuelita. After a moment of silence, my grandmother says.

*"Lo qué será, será.* I guess that's the way it must be."

Holy rollers, Batman! I'm guessing no one is arguing because Abuelo Sabino is sick. That's the reason we came to Juárez. My great-grandfather is in the hospital.

I never thought anything good would come of it.

# III

## 31 KATALINA

### "¡Qué descaro!"

DON SABINO ALWAYS smiled when he handed each of the children a peso on Sundays.

"*Niños bonitos.*" He would add, "These children are smart, too."

Don Sabino never says negative things about people, although he hates automobiles. He considers them dangerous and noisy machines to be avoided whenever possible. He prefers to walk everywhere and easily walks five miles to work each day. That's how the family discovered he was sick. He collapsed on the street after his legs failed him.

This morning at the hospital, we learned Don Sabino's time on earth is limited.

"*El cancer lo consume,*" the doctor told Doña Lucia and chastised her. "Why did you wait to bring him in?"

Even after the bad news, Don Sabino remains optimistic. "*Salúdame a Ramón,*" he said before we left the hospital. "Give my best to the boy."

The adults are now settled around the kitchen table in Amalia's home. Eduardo is leading a game of *lotería* for the kids, but Inez didn't want to play the Mexican version of bingo. She sits next to Amalia.

Patricia is by the stove preparing a meal. I'm surprised to see the old wood stove replaced by a shiny new appliance. Before I can remark on it, Doña Lucia cries out.

"*¡Medico pendejo!* That doctor is foolish! He spoke to me as if I knowingly waited until the cancer spread and it was too late to save my *viejito!*"

Doña Lucia is right, the doctor's an idiot. Medical checkups aren't cheap. A doctor's visit is a luxury.

Everyone is concerned about Don Sabino. That's probably why Amalia didn't argue about my decision to keep Inez home instead of allowing her to travel to San Agustin this year. Doña Lucia turns to Inez, as if reading my thoughts.

"Make sure you keep up your reading skills when summer comes," she says.

Inez leans against her grandmother. Amalia wraps her arms around my daughter. I appreciate Amalia's love of all my children. Nonetheless it's difficult to watch the close relationship between her and Inez. Will Inez and I ever share that kind of bond? Will I ever be able to ease my daughter's fears? I haven't even asked Inez about her experience with the FBI agents searching our house.

"Time to wash up for our meal," Patricia announces.

"Let the kids eat first so they can go out and play," Amalia suggests.

I agree, because the time has come to discuss business regarding *la cantina*.

The meal of *chile con carne* is scooped up with plenty of warm *tortillas*. The kids head outdoors as soon as they finish eating. It isn't long before the adults are also done with their meal. Patricia and I wash the dishes and then join the others at the table.

"Ramón wants to know why the *cantina* hasn't sold yet," I say.

"I'm doing my best." Emilio removes a cigarette from Amalia's pack of Faros.

"It's been almost three months. You said there had been some interest." I stop to light a cigarette. "What happened?"

"Don't you trust me, Katalina?"

"Are you spending the earnings of *la cantina*?" I blurt out without thinking.

"*¡Qué descaro!*" Amalia confronts me. "How dare you accuse my son of stealing when we are in agony over Sabino?"

"The tavern isn't a profitable business." Emilio quietly lights a cigarette.

"That's not what you've told people."

"The business belongs to Ramón!" Patricia grumbles.

"I'm Ramón's wife. *La cantina* is *our* business. I need money to feed my kids!" Frustrated, I snub out the cigarette I lit moments ago.

"Pay Emilio, then. He can't work for free just because they're brothers."

"Emilio told you, there is no money to give you, Katalina!" Amalia insists.

"Why didn't you feed the children with the money Alejandro gave you?"

Emilio's accusation stuns me. "That money was for Ramón's bail!"

"And my brother's still in jail!"

"You know there wasn't enough money to get him out, and you convinced me to spend some of it on repairs for *la cantina.* Emilio, I know you've taken from our home in the past. Now, you're taking from our business."

"*¡Atrevida!*" Amalia screeches. "You're so brazen! My boys were raised with values!"

"My husband is not a thief!" Patricia rises from the table and glares at me.

"Then tell me how you suddenly could afford to replace your old stove?"

Patricia gasps, "I can't believe what you're saying."

"I can't believe your husband is harming his brother's family!"

"No one forced Ramón to do what he did!"

"So, Ramón brought this on himself, and now you can ignore his children?"

"I would never abandon my children," Amalia says. "You're the one who moved them away from their home!"

"This was never their home!"

Amalia's sobbing almost drowns Doña Lucia's whisper.

"*Lo siento, Katalina,*" she murmurs. "I'm sorry you are suffering."

I turn to Amalia. "I'm sorry you've forgotten you have two sons, and that one of them needs you." I get up from the table to go gather my kids. "I'm disgusted with all of you. I won't be bullied anymore!"

The children return to say goodbye to their relatives. Inez gives me an accusatory glance when she sees Amalia crying. My daughter is young. She's aware only of things that bother her. She fails to notice that no member of the Ramirez family stops us from leaving.

# ▌▌▌

## 32  KATALINA

**My sister said what I need is an ally.**

RAMÓN'S ABSENCE HAUNTS me. Everything calls out his presence: his toothbrush when I brush my teeth, his clothing when I'm choosing a dress from the closet. I haven't seen him in weeks because every visit means lost wages. Fortunately, we write to each other. His letters arrive so frequently I can barely keep up with them.

I rip open the envelope the postman just delivered. Ramón's flawless penmanship greets me:

*Querida Katalina, I hope you and the children are well. The possibility of losing Abuelo Sabino while I sit in jail is obscene. He provided solace with his friendship. Thank you for checking in on my mother and the family. Regarding my case, Ralph Torres has some new information. He will be calling you soon. Until the next time, Ramón.*

My husband's salutation includes a term of endearment, but one word is always missing from his closing: "love."

I toss the piece of paper aside. Ramón is right: he will never see his *abuelo* again. I just returned from the hospital. Don Sabino is dying, *pobre viejito.*

Ramón knows nothing of my confrontation with the Ramirez family. He always defends his mother and brother, even when they hurt him. My sister Chayo said what I need is an ally. She found one: Tomás, a friend of the family and a high-ranking detective in Juárez.

Last week, Tomás escorted me to *la cantina*, leading the way into the dark tavern. Women are a rare sight in *cantinas*, and ladies never enter alone.

A group of customers enjoying the soft edge alcohol gives hard lives turned to watch us when we walked in. A blanket of haze hovered in the room from too many cigarettes. Behind the bar, neon signs advertised a variety of beers. The owner of the business rushed to meet us. Tomás projects authority and makes no excuses for looking official.

"*Lo siento*," the owner apologized after explaining that he had paid my brother-in-law for the lease of the building and the purchase of equipment.

"When did this happen?" Tomás asked.

"Two, maybe three weeks?" the chubby man replied. The smoke from his cigarette slowly twirled in the air until it disappeared into the hazy room.

"Emilio had no right to do this!" I said.

The man apologized again and insisted that I take up the matter with Emilio.

"He's right," Tomás agreed when we left the building. "I suggest you press charges against your brother-in-law."

I pick up Ramón's letter. He may get upset when he finds out Tomás accompanied me to the tavern, but he'll never forgive me if I turn a family dispute into a legal matter. My conscience stirs; I'll mention Tomás to Ramón in my next letter.

Ralph Torres has already contacted me. The attorney

explained the judge had denied his request for a separate trial from the other members of the drug ring. Apparently, Ramón was the only suspect not charged with possession. Now the prosecutor can use possession against him.

"I was counting on it for our defense," Ralph said. "Ramón's release now depends on the outcome of the trial. If we find any discrepancies with the handling of evidence or surveillance, it could reduce his sentence."

It was impossible to add money to the two-thousand dollars Alejandro gave me for Ramón's bond. That's why I gave Emilio money for repairs to *la cantina*. I also offered to pay Ralph Torres for his services, but he said public defenders were forbidden to accept money from clients. I can't mention any of this to Ramón in my letters.

The rest of the money paid our rent, but that's already due again. There's nothing to do but work long hours to pay the household expenses. The phone rings as I light a cigarette. I'm the only one home and take my time answering the call.

"Hello?"

"*Hola*, Katalina," Tomás greets me. "Am I calling at an inopportune moment?"

I chuckle. "You caught me lighting a cigarette."

"*Cigarrillos*, not good for your health," Tomás teases. "I'm calling to ask if you want to have lunch to discuss other options regarding your business."

I hesitate. My husband is the only man I've met for lunch in years—and yet why should there be concerns about a business meeting?

"I would like that very much," I tell Tomás.

# III

## 33 INEZ

**"Muchacha, you possess the soul of an elder."**

THE GLOSSY VENEER of Abuelo Sabino's coffin shines when a ray of sunlight pours through the window. The furniture in Tío Emilio and Tía Patricia's bedroom was removed to fit the casket. A group of women sit around murmuring rosary prayers. The air smells of votive candles and flowers.

On the way here, I asked Mamá why the ceremony was being held at Abuelita's house. She said this is how memorial services are performed in San Agustin.

"But the family lives in Juárez now!" I argued.

"It's important to maintain rituals, particularly when they involve mourning," she explained.

Abuelita Amalia starts bawling when she sees us. "*Gracias a Dios*, my children are here in my hour of need!"

Mamá sits next to Amá Lucia who looks sad and tired. Beside her is Tía Conchita, Abuelo Sabino's sister who traveled from Mexico City to bury her brother in Juárez.

Funerals don't frighten me. I've been to a few, never of a loved one. I walk over to the open coffin to see Abuelo Sabino.

Abuelo looks nothing like the man I remember smiling

and squatting with a stack of cactus pears on hot summer days. He would patiently peel the prickly skin of the refreshing treat while we kids waited impatiently.

The voices of the women in the prayer group rise and fall as they end their prayer.

"How is Ramón?" Tía Conchita asks Mamá. She looks just like her brother, but it's Conchita's quiet way that reminds me most of Abuelo.

"Ramón is struggling with Don Sabino's passing."

"It must be difficult, everything happening to your family."

"Everyone is suffering," Abuelita Amalia says, without looking at my mother.

Kids aren't supposed to notice when adults are mad at each other, but I know the bigger the fight, the more they try to hide it. The only thing I need to know today is why the people I love keep leaving.

"Some things just can't be explained, *mi'ja*," Amá Lucia says smiling.

How does Amá always know what I'm doing or thinking? Like the other day when she told me to read during summer vacation. Who told her I haven't bothered to renew my library card?

I go outside. My brothers and cousins are hanging out with some other kids. Every time we start playing, an adult hollers for us to be quiet. We keep trying until Eduardo hollers, "The hearse is here!"

I run inside in time to hear Abuelita shriek, "Sabino, your time is here!" She then promptly passes out.

Tío Emilio catches his mother before she hits the ground. The mourners cross themselves as Abuelo Sabino's casket leaves the house.

I hold my breath. Will Abuelo go to heaven even if he never went to church?

# III

## 34 RAMÓN

**Will I become a memory my children forget?**

PERHAPS AS MEN we take advantage of myths to avoid doing things we really don't want to do. Like pretending to be bad at housework or at expressing our feelings. I've never had a problem voicing my needs, but asking for comfort is difficult.

The death of Abuelo Sabino hit me hard. He was the only male influence in my life. A visit from Katalina and the family would have helped. I try to understand the reasons no one came to see me.

When I was enrolled in the military academy in Torreón, Abuelo visited frequently. We took long walks along the banks of the Nazas River, a temperamental body of water known for periods of droughts or flooding. In the rainy season, our feet sank into the muddy banks bordering the cotton fields that stretched for miles on both sides of the river. During our strolls, I shared stories about school life with the quiet man.

"Every morning at six o'clock we exercise and then practice military routines for three hours. On weekends we clean up the grounds."

"Do you enjoy your studies?" Abuelo asked.

"*Si, señor*," I answered, adding, "but the teachers are too strict."

"Tough rules turn boys into men," Abuelo assured me.

I never mentioned the fear tactics and bullying criticisms applied by our educators.

Someone once said you die when there is no one left to remember you. Abuelo Sabino's memory will live inside me forever.

This morning I share the loss of my Abuelo with only one inmate in my cell, Francisco. He and the scrawny brat who mocked my accent are the only inmates left from the original group that was here when I arrived three months ago. The older gentleman's temperament is a lifesaver among the riffraff.

Francisco offers me a cigarette. "Sorry about your loss," he says, lighting a match.

I thank him for his words and the cigarette.

"How's your wife?" he asks.

I look around the cell to see who's listening. The new inmates pretend to be busy.

"My wife's having a hard time."

"Most women do, at first, but women are survivors. It's their tears that confuse us. They cry through good and bad times. Once they overcome fear, you can't stop them. Don't worry, Ramón. You too will survive the chaos."

"What do you mean?"

"You'll survive the madness of prison life because you get it. Do the crime and do the time. You'll make a good recovery. Only the scars in your soul will remain, tucked away where no one can see them."

"What are you, a poet or a psychologist?" I tease. "I can never tell the difference."

"I speak from experience. Let me give you a little advice. Toss it if you wish. Be ready for your family to move on. They must and will." Francisco moves toward his bunk bed, then turns to me smiling. "I miss my kids like I miss the sun stroking my skin."

"*Poeta,*" I chuckle, snubbing out my cigarette. "Definitely a poet."

"Here we go again," the scrawny brat cries out. "Fucking *mojados* boring me with your conversation. Next time move to the other side of the room where I can't hear you."

Mexicans give nicknames to people to describe a physical characteristic or habit. If we like the person, the name is flattering. If we dislike them, nicknames can be insulting. The brat's nickname *El Mocho* was supposedly given to him because his physique appears to have been cut short at puberty.

"*Niño malcriado.*" Francisco teases El Mocho about his manners.

"I'm no fucking *niño!*" El Mocho screams. "I'm a man, and you can go fuck yourself, *abuelo!*"

I lunge at the kid and punch his stomach. One blow and El Mocho collapses on the ground. He tries to get up but I kick his head. It strikes the floor with a bang. He takes a few seconds to recover. When he gets up, El Mocho tries to punch my face. I lean back, then punch him in the stomach again. El Mocho bends over and falls to the ground. This time he stays down.

"*¡Pendejo!*" I scream. "If you can't respect yourself, at least respect your elders!" Adrenalin pumps through my body. My fists remain clenched, ready to fight anyone willing to come to El Mocho's defense. The men around me stand still.

Francisco dashes to the door and looks out the window. He shakes his head, indicating no guards are in the hallway. El Mocho stands up. A bruise is already developing on the left side of his mouth. He walks toward his cot without arguing.

My hands ache. I stare at the red knuckles.

"*Órale ese*," an inmate snickers. "Hey, man, you finally shut that boy's mouth."

My heart is still pounding as I stretch out on my cot. You reap what you sow, I think, turning toward the wall.

The hot air feels heavy. Francisco's words remain in my head. Katalina has the right to start anew, but I want the opportunity to get to know my children, the boys as men and Inez as a woman. I'm from a generation of men who left child rearing to women. Right or wrong, I know that if you don't participate you miss out on the experience.

Am I too late to right a wrong? Will I become a memory my children forget?

# spring 1967

# III

## 35  KATALINA

### A humiliating revelation for any woman

THE BODY CRAVES attention, longs for intimacy. It's not simply the need for sexual release, but a deep yearning for the touch of another human being. My thoughts flicker as the needle scrapes my finger. I yank my hand from the machine to avoid piercing it.

"*Cuidado, Katalina.*" Jimmy rushes to my side. "Are you okay?"

I nod, turning off the equipment. The lunch bell starts ringing.

"Do you have a minute?" he asks.

"Not really," I say, standing up from my machine.

"I'd like to see you after work." Jimmy moves toward me and whispers, "Let me ease your loneliness." His breath brushes my ear.

His voice never sounded so inviting. My fingers quiver when I place them on his chest to push him away. His firm body leans forward, touching my skin. My heart races as our eyes meet.

It takes a second, but I regain my wits. What am I doing,

jeopardizing my job and my children's welfare for a moment of fantasy with a kid?

"*¡Basta!*" I snap, removing my apron. "Stop it, Jimmy. We're married people—and your wife is pregnant, for goodness sake!"

"I can't change my feelings, Katalina."

"You *can* change them and you *must*."

"I have feelings for you both," he insists.

"*Disparate*, nonsense!"

Ramón once said the same thing to me about a mistress, a humiliating revelation for any woman.

### III

ROSIE IS EMPLOYED by Fisher Slacks, Inc., but she has a side business: offering small loans to anyone willing to pay her interest. Pawnshops and Rosie: neither hold financial ruin like foreclosure against me.

It makes me cringe, conducting business in the workplace cafeteria, but I paid the rent by hocking my fine jewelry. Now the utility bills are due, and there's little money left for food. Emilio spent all the money he received from *la cantina*. At least his family got a new stove from the deal.

"*Hola, Katalina.* Sit down and tell me what you need."

"Hello, Rosie. Would you please explain your terms?"

Rosie smiles. "People never bother with such details. How much do you need?"

"I need…fifteen dollars." Borrowing half my weekly salary makes me wince.

Rosie explains her terms while I pretend the information

makes a difference. Without hesitation, she counts out the money from a leather pouch.

"You can pay me back on the seventeenth."

"But that's two weeks after the due date."

"I'll worry about that." Rosie leans forward to whisper, "You know you're eligible for public assistance."

I've always considered those services for shiftless people. It's bad enough we're receiving Ralph's services for free. Rosie notices my uneasiness.

"How long have you worked at Fisher Slacks?" she insists.

"Fourteen years."

"You've paid taxes for fourteen years. Don't you know those taxes fund public assistance? Your children must eat. At least apply for food stamps, even if welfare won't pay your rent."

Rosie is right. My children need to eat.

After thanking Rosie, I make my way out of the cafeteria. A group of women sit at a table by the exit. Angelina, that vulgar woman who never misses a chance to insult me, sits with them.

"Look at her now, begging like the rest of the common people," she taunts. "What did you do with all the money your pusher husband made from selling weed?"

Some of Angelina's friends gasp, others giggle. I wonder if the lump in my throat is visible. My stomach churns as I approach my workstation and see Jimmy standing by my machine. Without thinking, I scoot in the opposite direction.

If Jimmy comes near me, I'll fall into his arms and weep.

# III

## 36 KATALINA

**Supervise your kids or...**

CARLITOS AND INEZ are the only ones home when I walk into the house.

"Where's Eduardo?" I ask.

"I don't know." Carlitos gets up to change the channel on TV.

"It's almost 6:30. He should be home by now." My patience wears thin. After a long workday I still have to cook dinner.

The front door swings open as I start toward the kitchen.

"Holy...!" Carlitos hollers.

"What happened to your hair?" Inez asks.

Eduardo stands by the door, rubbing his head.

"Watkins cut it. He said long hair is against school policy."

"That bastard almost shaved it off!"

"¡Carlitos!" I chide my son for using bad language. "Shut off the television!" I turn to Eduardo. "¿Quien es Watkins?"

"Watkins is the wrestling coach at school. He said I was beginning to look like a girl. My hair barely touched my shirt collar!"

"Watkins is a rude dude," Carlitos says in English.

Eduardo continues, almost whispering, "He took me into the locker room and clipped my hair with clippers then made me return to class."

What a cruel thing to do to a teenager! They're so sensitive about their appearance.

"The coach said…" Eduardo lowers his voice and his shoulders slump. "He said his students won't look like delinquents just because they have delinquent parents."

"*¿Qué?*" A chill runs through my body as the words seep through my brain. What have we done to our children? My heart breaks for my son but I don't know what to say to comfort him.

"Jerk!" Carlitos screams.

"Your hair will grow back," I assure Eduardo. Those are the only words of encouragement I can offer. I'm upset and angry, not at the coach but Ramón.

"That's *it*?" Carlitos cries out. "That's all you're going to say about it?"

"What am I supposed to do?" I snap.

"Call the principal. Report coach Watkins!"

"And tell the principal what?"

"That Coach Watkins is a jerk!"

"Yes, tell him the coach is a jerk!" Inez says.

"Do you think they'll listen to my complaint if Eduardo violated school policy?" I turn to Eduardo. "Why didn't you tell me you needed a haircut?"

"Now it's my fault?"

"No, Eduardo, but I need your help!"

Carlitos rolls his eyes. "Anything else we can do for *you*?"

"Stop being rude!" I pause to take a deep breath. "I need all of you to help me."

I don't understand my children's hostility. Ramón lost our home, put the family in jeopardy, and now sits in jail, yet I'm the one causing havoc for overlooking the added responsibility of getting the boys haircuts!

I'd laugh if Coach Watkins's message wasn't loud and clear: Supervise your kids or someone who doesn't care about their feelings will.

# III

## 37 KATALINA

**I've worked hard to stay out of housing projects.**

STEAM RISES AS I lift the iron off my blouse and remove the garment from the ironing board. The pot of boiling beans also releases steam into the kitchen. The warm room and the earsplitting sound of the television in the living room make me holler, "Turn it down!"

The loud chatter of the weatherman continues, echoing through the house: "The southwest desert blooms as wild goats graze on the Franklin Mountains. But today spring feels like summer, so our little lizard friends better scurry on the desert floor to find shade!"

"Better yet, turn that thing off!" I scream.

"I'm going out!" Inez hollers after shutting off the TV.

"Inez, come peel these potatoes!"

My daughter saunters into the kitchen. I ignore her glare and press a pair of the boys' slacks. Teenage mood swings, erupting hormones or a changing body—whatever it is, Inez is trying my patience. My friend Lupita is convinced Inez's behavior is a result of her encounter with the FBI agents. I think it has to do with her not visiting Amalia. The kids have only seen the Ramirez family a couple of times since Don Sabino's funeral over a month ago.

"I didn't hear you ask for permission to go out. Did you hem the dress you're wearing to school tomorrow?"

"You said you'd do it for me."

"I said you have to learn to do these things yourself."

"I'll hire someone to hem my dresses."

"*¡Basta!* I won't stand for bad manners."

Inez huffs and rolls her eyes. "I'll do it when I return."

"You'll fix the dress before you go out."

"What difference does it make if I fix it now or later?"

"It may be too late when you return."

"And it'll be too late to visit my friends if I do it now!"

"Inez, stop being difficult." I grab a hanger for the blouse I just pressed. "Don't forget, you're going with me to *el mercado* on Sunday."

"Why can't we shop at Safeway like normal people? Why do we have to shop in Juárez and why can't Eduardo or Carlitos go with you?"

"Because shopping is women's work," Carlitos says as he enters the kitchen.

"It's always women's work when men don't want to do it!" Inez hollers.

"Stop it, you two! Inez, you're going with me and that's that, you hear me?"

"I hate *el mercado!*"

The kitchen feels stuffy. I open the back door as the phone rings. Carlitos answers it.

"Hello?" he stands listening. "It's for you, Mamá." He hands me the phone and on his way out, smirks at Inez.

She stomps off to her bedroom without peeling the potatoes.

Jennie Ruane, a representative from the Department of Social Services, is on the phone. I took Rosie's advice and visited the agency two weeks ago.

Miss Ruane and I met in a depressing office space filled with rows of orange vinyl chairs and bright fluorescent lighting. The social worker sat behind a desk piled high with manila folders. Her questions annoyed me.

"Are your children still in school?"

"Of course," I responded.

"Sometimes children are forced to drop out of school under these circumstances."

"My children won't do that."

Miss Ruane's perky voice still annoys me even now that I'm at home.

"Hello, Mrs. Ramirez, this is the follow up call I promised when you left my office." Jennie pauses. "I thought you should know."

"What is it?"

"Your salary disqualifies you for welfare."

"I don't understand."

"Your salary exceeds the federal guidelines by five dollars," Jennie explains. "You do, however, qualify for food stamps."

"Five dollars, how is that possible...?" I stop speaking. Despair sounds so desperate.

"Perhaps if you move to a less expensive home," Jennie suggests.

"I've worked hard to stay out of housing projects."

"I didn't mean that," Jennie stammers. "What I meant—"

"Thank you, Miss Ruane, but we don't need your help."

The humiliation of being rejected by a system I detest makes me slam the receiver down on its cradle.

It's unfair to lash out at Miss Ruane. She's not to blame for the loss of my dream house, the one I dreamt of while sleeping on dirt floors as a child in San Agustin. When my fantasy came true it had tile floors, shiny new faucets, and a lawn I seeded and nurtured until green grass sprouted.

I recall the day after receiving the notice of foreclosure. It took everything to fight the urge to tear out my rose garden. Roses of every color taunting the tumbleweeds tumbling in the desert behind our house. With a shovel, I gently pulled every rosebush from the ground and donated my plants to neighbors. We would be renting and I was not decorating a building that wasn't my home.

Miss Ruane doesn't understand. I lowered my expectations once. It's not happening again.

III

## 38 KATALINA

**Only a father can protect a girl from lewd mockery.**

EL MERCADO CUAUHTÉMOC in Juárez is always open for business. This allows me to shop in El Paso on Saturdays, and shop in *el mercado* on Sundays after church. The two-story building buzzes with activity. Stalls stacked high with fresh fruits and vegetables line the sidewalks with color and texture from a variety of produce. Inside, the aroma of tacos sizzling in hot oil mingles with the herbs of *los curanderos* who sell their wares in the basement.

Today, I have no need for herbal teas or remedies. Inez and I stroll the ground floor. The loud voices of vendors echo through the building: *¡Frijole! ¡Arroz! ¡Papas!* Heaps of burlap bags containing grains stand beside wooden crates overflowing with root vegetables.

Refrigerated counters display fresh eggs and a variety of cheeses. Slabs of beef hang from the ceiling next to rows of sausage links and plucked poultry. Butchers slice and quarter meat while women shoo away the flies with paper flyswatters. The air smells of blood and bone marrow.

I prefer buying meat at Safeway, but I get more for my

dollar in Juárez. Inez and I leave the meat department and continue to the fresh vegetable section. I stop at one of the stands to inspect the selection.

"*¿Qué gusta, señora?*" a vendor asks.

I order chiles, onions, and potatoes. The vendor folds three cones from sheets of newspaper, one for each vegetable, wraps them up, and hands me the packages. I drop them in our shopping bag and pay him. Inez and I shop at *el mercado* for an hour.

On the way out, we approach a stand selling *taquitos*. A group of male vendors waiting in line ogle Inez.

"Can I have some?" she asks, gesturing toward the rolled corn tortillas stuffed with pork and garnished with cilantro.

"You can have my *taquito, mamita.*" One of the men leans so close to Inez, she winces. "My *taquito* is stuffed with so much meat you can barely fit it in your mouth."

The men laugh and yelp. I'm no stranger to lecherous comments that intimidate women and upset girls. The best thing to do is keep quiet.

"I hate this!" Inez snaps at me. "Why do you make me come here?"

"*Bella,* I'll make you feel so good you will come back every Sunday!" the man says without missing a beat. His friends laugh louder.

"Keep moving!" I shove Inez away from the crowd. Feeling helpless, I offer her a fruit drink. "Do you want a glass of *agua fresca* before we leave?"

"No! I want out of here. Don't you get it?"

"Being rude doesn't help."

Inez stomps off, but quickly returns. She looks frustrated and frightened.

I curse Ramón. Only a father can protect a girl from lewd mockery.

# III

## 39 INEZ

**We didn't even bump noses.**

ABUELITA AMALIA IS amazing! I never knew my grandmother could sew such cool clothes. She made dresses for me when I was little but they were all lace and petticoats. My new outfit is Mod to the core. We saw it in the window of The Popular department store in downtown El Paso the last time we visited Papá.

"I think it's a Mary Quant fashion," I told my grandmother and made such a fuss Abuelita took out a pencil to sketch the dress on a paper bag.

A few days later, she presented her creation: a perfect replica of a mannish shirt in a pattern of red dots on a white background. The shirt attaches to a miniskirt of white stripes on a red background. The necktie matches the skirt, the white hip-hugger belt is the same color as my white stockings, and my white patent leather shoes complete the outfit—perfect for tonight's party at Rudy's.

When I asked Mamá if I could attend, she immediately agreed. I think she feels bad about what happened on our visit to *el mercado* last time I went with her. I don't really hate shopping in Juárez. What's creepy is men gawking at my body, saying stupid things. I don't even know what they're talking about.

It doesn't bug me now. I'm having too much fun dancing at Rudy's party. He's the only kid I know whose parents don't mind when his friends come over. Maybe it's because we all fit in their big basement. The crowded room has only two pieces of furniture: a table for the record player and one in the corner holding snacks and sodas. The low ceiling is lit up with Christmas lights. There isn't any more room on the dance floor because Mitch Ryder and the Detroit Wheels are rocking the cinderblock walls: *Devil with a blue dress, blue dress, blue dress, devil with a blue dress on!*

"Groovy!" someone hollers when the music stops.

The sisters like Rudy's parties because he invites kids from other schools. I don't know my dance partner, but we nod to each other before leaving the dance floor. Laura's already at the refreshment table munching potato chips. We agreed to make the table our meeting place. Liz arrives and starts scolding her sister.

"What are you doing?!" she asks.

"I'm eating," Laura sputters as she chews. "Something wrong, princess?"

"Yes! Girls don't eat at parties!"

"That's stupid," I say. "Why put food on the table if you can't eat it?" I munch on a chip just to annoy Liz.

"It's not that you can't eat—never mind. You two just don't get it! I'm going to the bathroom to fix my hair."

A slow ballad starts playing.

"Wow, who's that?" Laura gestures toward the basement stairs.

I turn around and my gaze meets dark eyes lined with thick lashes. The lush brown hair of the boy at the bottom of the stairs brushes the collar of his white shirt. I look away to catch my breath.

"Hey, look who else is here." Laura gestures toward the entrance again.

Mona and Nicky must've come down the stairs when I looked away. Mona stares at us through the crowd, then grabs Nicky's hand. They walk toward the dance floor. Good, they're staying away.

"Where are all these kids from?" I wonder.

"Most are from *La Tech*," Laura says.

My brothers attend the Technical Vocational High School. How cool if I'm at a party with some of their friends.

"So, what's cooking?" Liz asks when she returns from the bathroom.

"Mona and Nicky just arrived," Laura says.

"Where are they?"

Laura points to the dance floor. That's when I notice the boy who took my breath away, walking toward us. My heart pounds. Is he really stopping in front of me?

"Wanna dance?" he asks.

I turn to my friends. Are they watching this? I've had cute boyfriends but this guy's gorgeous. Laura and Liz shy away.

"The song's almost over," I mumble.

"When this song ends, there will be another." His perfect teeth match his smile. "So, you wanna dance?"

I nod. Liz and Laura start whispering as soon as we leave. The boy finds a spot among the couples clinging to each other.

"What's your name?" he asks, pulling me close to his body.

"Inez."

"I'm David."

A whiff of English Leather cologne, the fresh scent of sunlight and starch on his shirt, and the smell of Juicy Fruit gum on his breath stir something inside me. The song ends too quickly. I pull away from David's arms, embarrassed by my desire.

Groovy! James Brown's voice bursts through the speakers.

"Wanna dance some more?" David asks.

I nod and start bopping with the kids around me. Cool, David is a good dancer. There's nothing more embarrassing than dancing with someone who has no rhythm.

"Open a window!" someone hollers, but no one leaves the dance floor.

That includes David and me. We dance to James Brown and keep dancing, through ballads, soul music, whatever is playing until the host makes an announcement.

"Last dance, last chance, with an oldie but goodie," Rudy calls out.

David reaches out for me when a slow ballad begins. He tightens his grip around me. How exciting! We barely move on the dance floor. David's scent, now musky with sweat, makes me want to touch every part of his body. I raise my head to wrap my arms around his neck and that's when it happens.

The flavor of salty potato chips and Juicy Fruit gum is united!

The touch and taste of his lips is delightful. David moans, kissing me and pressing his body against me. His private part hardens—it's frightening! I pull back without letting go of him. The music must've stopped because I hear Liz.

"Come on, Inez! We're leaving."

The magical moment between David and me turns awkward.

"I gotta go."

"I'll see you around," David says with a smile.

### III

THE FRESH AIR outside makes me feel good. All the kids are still hanging out, nobody wants to be the first to leave. A car crammed with teenagers finally pulls away from the curb.

"Groovy party!" someone screams through the window as the car takes off.

"That guy sounds like a stomper," Liz mocks. "Who says groovy? *Cool* is the word."

"That party was cool," Laura taunts her sister. "Lots of cute boys, and Inez got the cutest of all."

I blush and look around, hoping to see David, still wondering why he chose me. It has to be this lucky outfit. And how did we do it, breathing and kissing all at once? We didn't even bump noses.

"So, who is he?" Liz asks as we start the walk home.

"His name is David," I beam.

"What school does he go to?"

"I don't know."

"You danced with him all night, and you didn't ask?"

"Inez's mouth was a little busy," Laura teases. "Who cares what school he's from? The way these two were kissing, I thought they'd start a fire."

"He's a good dancer," I whisper. "That's all."

"Yeah, right, a good dancer," Laura giggles. "The best

part, Mona was there to see you don't need her stinking boyfriend. So why didn't Mona and Nicky come over?"

"They only hang out with each other," Liz says.

"Talk about boring," I remark.

"Yeah, no shit." Laura adds, "I'm glad Mona didn't stop by to bug us."

"I like Mona," Liz declares. "She's *my* friend."

"Of course she is. That's why she stays away."

"You are such a bitch!" Liz screeches.

For once I'm glad to hear the sisters' chatter. The dark street would be scary without it.

Side streets aren't well lit so the house with all the lights on really stands out. I prod Laura with my elbow as we near it and gesture to a blond teenage boy standing on the porch, lighting a cigarette.

"Hey, guys!" he calls out. "Come look at this!"

Two boys join him at the doorway, and they start whistling.

"Love those miniskirts!" one of them hollers.

An older boy appears behind them. He looks us over.

"Forget it, they're fucking Mexicans! Fucking wetbacks are everywhere, rolling across the desert like tumbleweeds, fat and ugly!" His friends laugh and follow the boy inside.

"And stompers are assholes!" Liz cries out.

"Shut up!" Laura scolds her sister.

"Yeah, well, those guys are assholes!" Liz rages.

"Yeah, and your mouth is going to get us in trouble!"

Suddenly, the brightly lit house is scarier than the dark street in front of us. We continue walking in silence.

"We'll see you tomorrow," Laura says when we reach the corner where we part ways.

"Tomorrow we'll have fun again," I tease, but no one giggles.

The sisters live two blocks away, a short distance during the day but at night every shadow makes my heart pound. I never worry about walking home alone when we're having fun. Tonight, the memory of the angry boy's voice creeps me out more than the darkness. He made the word Mexican sound so dirty.

Sticks and stones break my bones, and words hurt, hurt, hurt me. I wanted to scream out like Liz, but I wasn't mad. His words made me sad.

I remember the time my friends Linda and Sylvia asked Beverly, one of the Negro girls at school, if we could touch her hair. Beverly looked sad when we acted like we were touching something strange.

I promise never, ever to ask to touch anyone's hair again.

## III

## 40 KATALINA

**A silly response to a serious accusation.**

I WAIT BY THE door as Inez dashes up the porch steps.

"You're late," I declare as soon as she walks into the house.

"A little," Inez mumbles. Someone once wrote that they never met a better match for their energy than their child, always questioning, arguing, challenging. Inez challenges, questions, and argues.

"*Bastante*. It's almost eleven and you were supposed to be home by nine!"

"Ten!"

"*Qué paso?*" I ask. "You look frightened."

"Nothing."

"I hope your friends walked you home. You can't be out in the middle of the night."

"Why do you act like you care?"

"*¡Claro!* Of course I care. You don't understand. It's dangerous—"

"Are Eduardo and Carlitos home yet?"

"Boys can protect themselves. Besides, what will people say about you running around at night?"

"The same thing people say about you running around during the day."

"*¡Grosera!* Stop sassing me." My daughter's comment startles me. "I have no idea what you're talking about."

"Why haven't you taken me to *el mercado* again? Is it so you can meet that man you talk to on the telephone? You haven't even asked me."

Inez's remark feels like a blow to the head. My face feels hot and the dizziness makes my head ache.

"You...you don't like going to *el mercado*, remember?" A silly response to a serious accusation. I go on the defensive. "Tomás is helping me with—"

"I bet he's helping."

"Stop it! Tomás is helping me with the business in Juárez." I'm ashamed of lying—the business has already been sold—but Inez is trying my patience.

"Tío Emilio is helping you with that!"

"No, he's not." I look straight at Inez. At least this statement is true.

Inez studies me, the way she used to when she first came to live with our family in El Paso.

"What about Papá? Don't you care about my dad?"

"I'm doing this to help your father."

Inez frowns. She doesn't believe me.

Shamed and fatigued, I give my last command, "Go to bed, Inez. We'll discuss this in the morning. *Hasta mañana.*"

Inez leaves the room; I collapse on the couch. It's true. I enjoy having an adult who takes an interest in my opinion. Tomás is good company. He's married and not really my type, although I can't deny his tailored suits and high rank give him a distinguished look that's exciting. He also makes me feel important.

Men have always lusted after me. I need to feel like I matter, to know someone's life would be incomplete without me. Ramón made me feel special for a brief moment. Now even my kids resent me.

# III

## 41 INEZ

**Can't forget what my kisses did to his body.**

THE SISTERS AND I never again discussed the white boys on the porch. It pissed me off, though, the way they ruined my beautiful night with David.

It's been two weeks, three days, and four hours since I last saw David and I can't stop thinking about him. The other thing I can't forget is what my kisses did to his body. Would my kisses do the same thing to another boy? Maybe I'll find out tonight.

"I'm meeting this guy at school tonight," Liz said this morning, "I told him you two would be there so he's bringing a couple of friends."

"What?" we screeched.

"Stop being such babies," Liz scolded.

"Who is this guy and who are his friends?" I asked.

"Who cares? It'll be a gas."

"Only if his friends are cute," Laura said.

"They better be cute. Who wants to go out with an ugly dude?" I showed off the new word I learned from Carlitos.

"What's a dude, Inez?" Laura asked.

"A dude is a guy."

"Only one way to find out if these *dudes* are cute," Liz egged us on. "Coming or not?"

III

THE BOYS ARE already waiting in the school grounds when we arrive. It's hard to check them out in the dark. Once we're beside them, I see they're cute, but not gorgeous like David. Liz's boyfriend takes her by the hand and they quickly disappear into the shadows.

"What's your name?" one of the boys asks.

"I'm Inez, she's Laura."

"I'm Jesse and that's Tony."

"Do you want a cigarette?" Tony asks.

We nod. Tony hands us each a cigarette, then lights them for us.

Jesse turns to Laura. "You wanna take a walk?"

"In the dark?" I ask.

"Don't worry, we won't get lost."

Jesse's remark makes Tony laugh. I don't find it funny. Laura giggles when Jesse leads her away by the hand. It pisses me off because we agreed to stay together. Now she's leaving me alone with a strange boy in the dark.

"How about making out?" Tony asks.

Without knowing what to say, I draw hard on my cigarette. Before I have time to exhale, Tony grabs me, tosses my cigarette to the ground, and kisses me hard. The smoke and Tony's tongue almost gag me. The kiss is so different from David's, I don't like it.

Suddenly, Tony places his hand on my breast.

"Stop it!" I push him away.

"Come on," Tony snickers. "I know you like it."

"I do not!" I walk away more pissed off than ever. "You're a pervert."

Tony follows me.

"Don't come near me!" I holler.

"I'm sorry. I didn't mean to, but my friends said your friends—"

"Shut up!" I can't believe what Tony is suggesting.

The sisters wouldn't let someone touch them, would they?

# III

## 42 INEZ

**Snubbed by the snob sisters**

THE SPLENDOR OF spring is not straw-colored lawns turning into beds of emerald green. The best part of spring is that the end of the school year is near.

"Settle down, people!" Mrs. Rogers instructs. "There are only two weeks left in the school year so let us continue reading our essays on current events. Will someone remind us what a current event is?"

Sheldon raises his hand: "Something that takes place in the present, but affects the future. Like when the Beatles first appeared on the Ed Sullivan Show. You said the Beatles were a current event, but they changed music forever."

"Very good, Sheldon. Let me give you another example. Between 1945 and 1964 the birth rate of the United States increased dramatically. This increase, dubbed 'the baby boom,' was a current event. In fact, you are part of that generation and—"

"Who cares?" Laura mutters.

"Laura, have you something to add?"

"No, Miss."

"Then please stop mumbling." Mrs. Rogers continues. "Never have we seen such a large group of people coming of age at the same time. That's important because it gives you the power to make a difference in our country and the world. Your influence is already apparent. Pepsi-Cola dubbed you the 'Pepsi Generation,' and that means you are now a target of Madison Avenue."

Sometimes I don't get what Mrs. Rogers says. Like, where is Madison Avenue and who lives there? I raise my hand.

"Yes, Inez."

"Where is Madison Avenue, and do they only drink Pepsi there?"

Mrs. Rogers smiles, "That's a good question, Inez. Has anyone heard of Madison Avenue?" Not a hand is raised. "Madison Avenue is in New York City. Some of the biggest advertising agencies are located there."

"What's an advertising agency, Miss?" Ricardo asks.

It's surprising that Mrs. Rogers doesn't scold Ricardo for not raising his hand. "These are businesses that produce commercials and ads to sell food and merchandise. Some ads use characters that I'm sure you all know. Let's see. There's the Maytag repairman, the Pillsbury Doughboy, and Charlie the Tuna. Not all advertising agencies are on Madison Avenue in New York. I suppose Madison Avenue has become a brand itself."

No one in the room says a word. We have a Maytag at home but Mamá never buys Pillsbury pastries or tuna. I wish she would.

"Are there any more questions about Madison Avenue?" Mrs. Rogers asks, looking around. "Okay, who wants to start reading today?"

I'm ready with my essay, but I don't want to be first.

"Mike, why don't you start?" Mrs. Rogers calls out.

Mike walks up to the front of the room. We stare because overnight Mike swapped his Buddy Holly glasses for a pair of John Lennon granny frames. Mike starts reading without looking at the class.

"My essay is on the Vietnam War. My brother Victor just graduated from high school and next month he will be shipped out to go fight in Vietnam. Dad says it's a disgrace that our government is sending Victor to fight someone else's civil war. Victor says it would be a bigger disgrace if he didn't go and help. The first American combat troops arrived in Vietnam in March of 1965. I don't know who's wrong or right but I'm proud of my brother Victor." Mike folds the piece of paper and turns to look at Mrs. Rogers.

"Thank you, Mike. It was an informative and touching essay. You may sit down." The teacher turns to the class. "How many of you know someone fighting in this war?"

Almost every student raises their hand.

"Mike is correct. Regardless of what side of the debate you're on, we should all be very proud of his brother Victor and the other men serving our country. Laura, you're next."

"I don't have it, Miss," Laura whispers.

"Why?"

"I didn't know what to write."

"Why didn't you ask me for help?" Mrs. Rogers scolds. "I told you before, you may not make it through the seventh grade. You need this final score!"

Laura's face turns red. No one says a word.

"Inez, you're next."

My heels click on the floor and my heart races on my way to the front of the class.

"My essay is on Twiggy," I announce.

*"Twiggy?"* someone mutters from the back of the room.

I start reading fast before I have time to chicken out: "Twiggy is an English model who is very Mod and very skinny. I like the minidresses Twiggy wears with tights. I like her haircut and the eyelashes she paints on the lower part of her eyes. I read that it took seven hours to cut and color her hair. I like Twiggy because she's young and Mod."

I turn to Mrs. Rogers when I finish reading. The teacher is busy writing so I walk quietly back to my desk.

"Twiggy is girly stuff," Sheldon teases when I sit down.

"Shut up," I whisper, smiling.

"Actually most designers of women's fashions are men." Mrs. Rogers stops writing and gets up from her desk. "The fascinating thing about Twiggy is that she was only sixteen when she signed her modeling contract last year. She's not much older than you. Remember our discussion about the baby boom? This is a perfect example of the impact of this phenomenon. The advertising industry is now targeting the youth of America, and that will give you a lot of power when you start earning and spending your own money."

I'm proud to have started such a smart discussion, until someone brings up Twiggy's breasts.

"Twiggy looks like a boy," one of the boys hollers. "Her flat chest!"

Everyone giggles. I swear they're all now staring at my breasts. Darn it, I should've picked a different subject.

"All right, class, settle down. We're out of time today, but we will continue reading our essays tomorrow. Get home safely."

As we leave class, Sheldon teases me again.

"Hey, Twiggy lover, you're weird!"

"Shut up," I reply with a smile.

"I'll take Sofia Loren anytime!" he hollers running off.

### |||

"MRS. ROGERS IS a bitch!" Laura hisses when we head out to the courtyard.

Liz is already waiting with Mona and the other girls.

"So where are you guys meeting boys once school ends and you can't meet up in the school grounds?" Mona asks.

"Why can't we meet in the school grounds?" Laura asks.

"Hanky-panky not allowed on school grounds during summer vacation," Mona laughs.

"Hanky-panky?" I look at Liz. Who else would tell Mona about us meeting those boys the other night?

"Now we know why boys like you," Mona says.

"Mona!" Liz sounds nervous and tries to laugh it off.

"Takes one to know one," I quip. I act like it's a joke, but Liz is creeping me out. What is she telling Mona, and why isn't Laura stopping her?

I remember Tony's remarks about the sisters. How would they feel if I told Mona what Tony said about them? Why is everyone acting like a jerk? I smile when my old friends Sylvia and Linda walk by.

"Hi!" I call out to them.

Sylvia and Linda ignore me.

"You've been snubbed by the snob sisters," Mona teases.

"Little girls," I say.

"Better a little girl than a slut!" Sylvia hollers. Her remark stings, the insult made worse by Mona's loud cackle.

The splendor of spring is looking forward to having a whole summer without Mona. That will be delightful!

summer 1967

# III

## 43 INEZ

**They can tell Papá stories about the
Wizard of Oz so he won't be lonely.**

THE FEDERAL COURTHOUSE in downtown El Paso looks like
a huge block of concrete standing under the June sun. There
are five floors, but only four of them have huge windows. The
roof is so flat you can barely see it.

Papá's court hearing started two weeks after school ended.
On the first day, we met Abuelita Amalia and Tío Emilio in
one of the two courtyards inside. They stood admiring a huge
painting that covered two walls.

"It's called a mural, not a painting," Carlitos said.

"'*Pass of the North*,'" Eduardo read from a plaque on the
wall. "It's 11 by 54 feet and completed in 1938 by Thomas C.
Lea, III." He then read the quote on the mural: "'O Pass of the
North, now the old giants are gone we little men live where
heroes once walked the inviolate earth.'"

"What does 'inviolate' mean?" I stared at the images of pi-
oneers standing side by side with a Mexican *charro*, a Spanish
Friar, American Indians, a *conquistador*, and cowboys. Behind
them are the barren peaks of what looks like the Franklin
Mountains and the vast desert around them.

My brothers didn't answer because Papá's trial was starting.

Today is the third day, and I dash up the front stairs by myself. Mamá and my brothers follow. I need to see the mural before anyone else arrives.

The beautiful images stare back at me. The desert scares me a little but I like the way people stand so straight and tall in the picture. I love the donkey standing behind the miner, its head peeking under the man's hand, looking right at me.

"*Anda, Inez!*" Mamá calls out when she and the boys finally enter the building.

"I'll be there in a minute."

When I turn around, Abuelita is watching me. I'm surprised to see her without Tío Emilio.

She smiles as I walk toward her. Abuelita searches in her purse and pulls out a bright yellow mango. She places a finger against her lips.

"*Shhh—no le digas a nadie,*" she says.

Manila mangos aren't allowed into the United States from Mexico, but Abuelita knows it's my favorite fruit. Every now and then she sneaks one across the border in her purse. I giggle, take the mango from her hand and place it in my bag.

"*¡Mi pajarito!*" Abuelita hugs me.

With my arm around her waist, we go into the courtroom. Mamá is talking to the attorney. He walks to the front of the room when they finish their conversation.

"They're sentencing Ramón today," Mamá tells my grandmother.

"*¡Dios mío!*" Abuelita trembles as I bury my head against her body.

Will I ever see Papá again? I release my grandmother.

We slide onto benches. Across the aisle is the family of Papa's friend Miguel.

The courtroom is lined with heavy wood paneling and tile floors. Two oversized crystal chandeliers hang from the ceiling. The air-conditioning cools the air, making it fresh and clean.

I'm glad we stopped to look at the beautiful mural, because as soon as the proceedings start—I learned that word from Papá's attorney—everyone gets serious. The whole thing reminds me of an episode of Perry Mason. The only thing missing is someone standing up to confess: "I did it! I'm the one!"

Papá sits up front with his back to us and hardly ever turns around. He and his friends dress up every day in suits and ties. Mamá said Papá is going to prison. How does she know that? I thought she was lying, until I saw the witnesses: U.S. Marshals with guns in holsters strapped to their waists, and FBI agents, all testifying against Papá and his friends.

My heart raced when the FBI agents who came to our house testified. I turned away so I didn't have to look at them.

The agents said one of the things they discovered about Papá is that he received frequent visits from Western Union. I swear they didn't hear that from me, though I remember the messengers. The first time one came around I thought someone had died. It turns out my dad was having money wired from Chicago. This doesn't make sense. If Papá was receiving money, we would've been rich.

I want to go up and hug dad, but Mamá told me we're not allowed to touch him. There's one thing we *have* to do: stand up whenever the judge enters or leaves the room. Eduardo said if we don't do it we could be arrested. Is that possible?

The bailiff makes an announcement: "Please rise for the Honorable Judge Elmer B. Huntington!"

Everybody stands. The judge walks in and settles into the black leather chair behind the bench. "You may be seated!" the bailiff hollers.

We sit. The sound of shuffling papers echoes through the room.

"Good morning," the judge says, looking at the people in the courtroom watching him.

The judge's bench reminds me of a pulpit. Usually, the judge looks like God watching from above. Today the judge looks like just another mean guy.

"The jury has arrived at a verdict, and I see no reason to postpone the inevitable." The judge picks up a piece of paper before continuing, "I'm prepared to read the verdict and set sentence this morning."

Gasps and whispers fill the room. Carlitos leans toward our mother. Eduardo also whispers in Abuelita's ear. Our grandmother makes the sign of the cross and leans against Eduardo. I fold my arms across my chest, hoping no one will touch me.

The bailiff orders the defendants to rise. Papá, his friends, and their lawyers stand up. My dad looks straight ahead, his friend Miguel looks at the floor, while their friend Roberto smiles at his lawyer.

The judge reads Miguel's name, then the charges. Miguel's son whispers to his mother. Finally, the judge calls out "Guilty!"

Miguel's wife's sobs ring out before she collapses in her son's arms. Abuelita Amalia wipes her tears. Mamá stares at the floor without making a sound. She looks scared. The judge does the same for Roberto, then I hear Papá's name.

"Ramón Ramirez!" the judge calls out.

I lean back on the bench. It's weird, but I feel nothing. A memory twirls in my head of Papá, Mamá, and me visiting a drive-in restaurant. The waitress locked the tray on the car window but Papá rolled it down accidentally. Food and glass splattered all over the pavement. I hid on the floor, embarrassed for the family and worried dad would get in trouble.

In the courtroom, Papá's still standing. He sways a little, like he's nervous. Is my dad scared? He gives us a quick glance and turns away. Is he ashamed to have us watching him?

The judge announces the sentence: "Each defendant is sentenced to fifteen years." Papá and his friends are handcuffed and led out of the courtroom.

Fifteen years! I lean forward on the bench. What did I do to my dad? Is he ever coming back? What will happen to our family? Slowly, I slide back and rest my head on the bench.

Papá's attorney whispers to my mother, "We think they'll be sent to the United States Penitentiary in Leavenworth, Kansas."

If Papá is going to Kansas maybe he'll meet Toto and Dorothy. They can tell Papá stories about the Wizard of Oz so he won't be lonely.

# III

## 44 RAMÓN

### No shortcuts in life

THE CITY OF Leavenworth, Kansas, is named for the Fort Leavenworth Military Reservation which sits on a high bluff overlooking the Missouri River. The military base is located on the north side of U.S. Highway 73, also known as Metropolitan Avenue. This road leads directly to the Leavenworth penitentiary.

*The huge limestone walls of the main cellblocks of the penitentiary extend east and west from a dome-capped Rotunda modeled after the U.S. Capitol Building in Washington, D.C. The Rotunda houses the guard tower and the Administration Building, and gives the prison its nickname of the Big Top.*

For the past two days I read everything I could about the Leavenworth penitentiary. Now, the words keep whirling in my head as the train we're riding pulls into Albuquerque. The El Paso Railroad Service reserved a car for our journey to Leavenworth. The railroad car is half-empty, though it won't be for long because the train just stopped to board more convicts.

The last couple of weeks were grueling. In the courtroom,

there was no more hiding my rash judgements, reckless behavior, and spending. I couldn't even look at my family as strangers unraveled illegal acts, questioning my ethics.

Yesterday, the family came to say goodbye. Mamá cried. Her tears reminded me of the day she delivered me to the military academy as a boy. This time there was no excitement, only fear and sadness. Katalina and my kids barely spoke. Had they grown so accustomed to my gallivanting that they couldn't gauge the severity of my departure?

I have injured my family and lost the freedom to live life on my terms. Most painful is knowing I probably won't see my grandmother again. If she survives, Amá Lucia will be old and weak, not the strong vital woman I remember. Truth is, I have no idea who will welcome me home.

Francisco was right: there are no shortcuts in life. He claimed our path is chosen for us, that we can enrich the journey but can't alter the outcome. Either way, I've made a decision not to change the rules of the game. My goal while serving my sentence is to reclaim my freedom and make amends to my family.

The train leaves the Albuquerque station, picking up speed as we approach the desert. The orange sun kisses the horizon.

I can't wait for the sun to stroke my face as a free man again.

# |||

## 45 **INEZ**

**Playing like you...**

GOOD THING PAPÁ'S trial took place during my summer vacation. It would've been torture facing my classmates, because on the day of his sentence Papá was on TV and the radio every time the news played. I made sure to watch and listen for his name.

Mamá returned to work the day after Papá's trial. We're still walking around the house without saying much. I'm not really up for going out but the sisters keep calling me to hang out at Memorial Park. We started doing that when school ended. Today's rain isn't going to let us.

Lightning marks the sky like scribbles on a piece of paper. The thunder above the plains of El Paso sounds like bowling balls rolling down the alley. The rain stops at four o'clock, our phone rings at 4:05.

"It's for you!" Carlitos calls out to me.

I stop vacuuming and take the phone from his hand.

"Ma is punishing Liz," Laura tells me. "She can't go out, but I'm not grounded and I can't take the boredom in this house another minute."

"I'll be right over." It takes seconds to put away the vacuum cleaner.

"Where are you going?" Carlitos asks as I dash toward the door.

"Swimming."

"They won't let you swim in the rain."

"It stopped raining."

"So where's your swim suit?" he asks.

I recall Liz's lecture: "Who wants to swim with a bunch of kids peeing in the water? The swimming pool is only cool for people-watching and to be seen." Liz made no sense but we stopped swimming anyway.

"We're going to hang out," I tell my brother.

"Last time you lie to me and I lie for you," Carlitos warns as I leave the house.

|||

I LOVE THE WAY the rain cleans the world and the sun makes it sparkle. Laura doesn't seem to notice. She's still talking about Liz being grounded.

"Ma hates when we talk back to her husband."

We approach the Copper Avenue entrance to Memorial Park. Lush trees and manicured lawns give it a touch of elegance. The tennis courts and swimming pool are separated by a lawn. We find a spot to sit on by the courts because they sit higher than the pool and offer the perfect view.

Laura runs her hand through the grass to make sure it's dry.

"Hey, look! Isn't that the girl who transferred right before school ended?" I gesture toward a girl getting out of the pool.

Her friends are splashing in the water. A couple of boys look on through the chain link fence surrounding the swimming pool.

"Her name is Rebecca. Everyone calls her KiKi," Laura explains and adds, "She's a friend of Mona's."

KiKi climbs the diving board and prepares to take the plunge. Her suit looks like the one worn by the James Bond girl in the *Dr. No* movie.

"She looks like she's swimming in her underwear and bra."

"Someone said KiKi's mom died," Laura whispers.

I feel like a jerk. Losing parents to divorce or prison stinks. A parent dying is scary.

"Oh my God, look, Inez! There's David!"

David is one of the boys flirting with KiKi's friends through the fence. Suddenly, he turns toward us and whispers to the boy beside him.

"Darn it, Laura, I think he heard you," I scold.

The boys start walking toward us. David is more gorgeous than I remember. His hair is longer, falling just below his neck, and the tails of his white shirt hang over dark pants. I turn away to stop from staring.

"Hey, what's up?" David stands over me smiling.

I take a deep breath before responding, "Nothing."

"So, what's your name again?"

"Inez."

"I'm David."

"Yeah, I remember." I yank a handful of grass from the ground. Now David knows I haven't stopped thinking about him.

David sits down beside me and rolls onto his stomach while introducing his friend. "That's Willy."

"This is Laura."

"Do you guys dance?" Willy asks.

"Yeah, we dance," Laura replies.

"Have you been to The Blue Cloud?"

"Not yet," I answer.

Laura stares at me. We have no idea what Willy is talking about, but I don't want the boys to think we're square.

"Oh, man, you gotta go—it's a gas! There're dances on Sunday afternoon if you can't go out at night."

"We go out at night," Laura says.

"Cool." Willy smiles and grabs her hand.

"How old are you?" David asks, sliding his finger along my arm.

"I'm fifteen," I fib. "And you?"

"Sixteen."

It feels like minutes since the boys arrived, but before we know it the lifeguard blows his whistle announcing closing time.

"Hey, you wanna take a walk?" David asks.

I nod. David jumps up and pulls me up from the ground. I tighten my grip around his hand. Without speaking, we make our way into the shadows of the park. Streetlights already glimmer in the distance.

|||

MY TONGUE FINDS the spearmint gum in David's mouth. The fresh, mint flavor bursts inside our mouths before he swallows it and pulls me down to the ground. His hand cups my breast, then his fingers unbutton my blouse. He slides one leg between mine and mounts my body. I gasp—his private part feels harder than the last time. What does it do? Will it hurt me?

David bites my neck and whispers in my ear. I don't hear him. His hair tickles my nose. Suddenly, he starts unfastening his trousers. His white briefs glow in the darkness, my heart pounds, then I hear the scream.

"Inez!" Laura hollers. "Inez, where are you?"

We freeze: no moves, no sounds.

"Inez!"

"I have to go," I whisper.

"No, please don't," David pleads. "I'll walk you home."

"Inez!" Laura screams again.

I push David off, he moans. I button my blouse.

"Can I see you tomorrow?" he asks, lying on the ground.

My eyes focus on Laura's silhouette in the distance. I leave without responding.

"Jeez, where were you, Inez?" Laura's hair looks wild. "What were you doing?"

"Playing, like you." I brush grass off her back. Laura giggles. "Are you all right?" I ask. "You sounded like an old woman hollering."

"Willy's too fast for comfort."

We laugh, but I'm frightened. I let David touch me and liked it.

No one must ever know how much I love him.

# III

## 46  KATALINA

**I couldn't imagine my world without her.**

**I** SIGH, PUSHING RAMÓN'S clothes aside to hang clean laundry. The suit he wore at the trial is now covered with plastic. My husband's gone, sentenced to fifteen years at the United States Penitentiary in Leavenworth, Kansas. *No sé*, I don't even know where Kansas is located. How much will a bus ticket cost to visit him? The lawyer Ralph Torres said Ramón would be eligible for parole in three years. I think that means he could finish his fifteen-year sentence at home, depending on his behavior in jail. Does a person's conduct change in prison?

I hear Inez come home and dash out of my bedroom to meet her in the living room. "*¿Donde andabas?*" I demand to know where she's been.

"Swimming."

"*¡No mientas, Inez!*"

"I'm not lying."

"It's eight o'clock. I know what time the pool closes." I

move closer to Inez and notice the mark on her neck. "What's that?"

"What?"

I drag Inez by the arm into my bedroom and place her in front of a mirror.

"*¡Eso!* That mark on your neck is vulgar!"

Inez smiles when I point it out. Is she proud of the hickey on her neck?

"You weren't raised like this!"

My daughter cringes, as if my words sting her ears. "You're right! You didn't raise me! Abuelita did when you left me in Juárez!"

I stutter, "I didn't leave you! Amalia—wanted—"

"Don't blame my grandmother! You're the one who didn't want me! You even forgot me in the trolley! I wish you had left me in Juárez!"

"You know nothing! Amalia forced—"

"Stop blaming people and stop cheating on my dad! Is that why you wanted him in prison?"

I've never struck my daughter before. Now my hand lands hard on her face.

"You feel better?" Inez smiles, tears well up in her eyes.

My body sways. I brace myself. My daughter must not see me crying.

"It's not true, Inez. I'm not cheating on your father, I swear."

"You're a liar!" Inez turns away rubbing her face and stomps off to her bedroom,

My body trembles. Yes, it *was* disappointing to discover I was pregnant with Inez, only because of Ramón's treachery.

The birth of another child complicated a departure. Once Inez was born, I couldn't imagine my world without her.

As far as Tomás is concerned, I'm enjoying the attention, the give and take of friendship that evolves into…romance?

Marriage is sacred. It's a union ordained to create children. Something so precious must be respected, and yet our emotions betray us. Is it wrong to long for someone to hold me?

Did Ramón ever feel the loneliness of a bed that once held two bodies?

# III

## 47 INEZ

**They were only dancing.**

THE FIRST TIME I heard the word *cholos*, I thought people were talking about *churros*, the tasty sugar and cinnamon fried bread sticks so popular in Mexico. Laura explains *cholos* are the boys who dress in khaki pants and white tank tops or flannel shirts. They wear hairnets or bandanas on their heads and have tattoos all over their bodies.

"The hairnets make those boys look like school cafeteria ladies," I say.

"*Cholos* belong to gangs with names like K14 and Los Monos," Laura adds.

"*Cholos* rule, Mods are dead!" Liz hollers.

"Yeah, okay," I say, applying more lipstick in front of the mirror in the sisters' bedroom. We're on our way to the Blue Cloud for the afternoon dance. Mamá said I was never going out at night again. Yeah, okay!

"Actually, hippies rule the world now," Yoli says. The older sister has become a snob always correcting us.

"Hippies look like they always need a bath," Liz says, "and they're potheads!"

The sisters grow quiet. No one mentions Papá, yet I know everyone is thinking about my dad. The only sound in the room is Tommy James singing on the radio: *Children behave, that's what they say when we're together, and watch how you play....*

"Turn off the radio," Liz says.

"Hold on, this song's a gas!" I love Tommy James, and I don't care who knows it.

"Let's go or we'll be late," Liz argues.

"Love, peace," Yoli says, lifting her hand and forming a V with two fingers. "Don't be late or you'll piss off mom."

III

DAVID'S FRIEND WILLY is right. The Blue Cloud is a gas! I've attended dances in halls for weddings and *quinceañeras*, always with adults. Here, even the DJ looks like a teenager. Kids of every age and color dance together, swaying like one huge body. The DJ keeps the music going with two turntables, starting a new song before the other ends. The music rattles the walls of the hall, which is really an old warehouse with the windows boarded up. I'm drenched in sweat, but can't stop dancing.

"Check this out, people!" the DJ hollers. "We're getting a sneak peek at a big hit and this beat cannot be weak because it's about to compete with the sexy voice of Mr. Marvin Gaye!"

Marvin's voice soars through the speakers: *O-o-o-oh, I bet you're wondering how I knew about your plans to make me blue....*

When Marvin finishes the song about his cheating girlfriend, I decide it's time for a break. My partner and I nod to each other before leaving the dance floor.

I recognize David's back as he huddles with friends.

Suddenly, the music stops and the overhead lights blaze so bright my eyes squint.

"All right, people," the DJ announces, "it's time for the big dance contest!"

The crowd cheers before clearing the dance floor. The DJ leaps off the stage, adjusting the collar of his Nehru jacket when he lands. The cord of his microphone trails behind him as he makes his way to the middle of the dance floor.

"Remember, this contest is for singles, so if you enter with a partner you'll be competing against each other and you don't want to do that. All right, then, let's get grooving with Otis and Carla and their latest hit from Stax Records. Sock it to 'em, Ponchy!"

As soon as the DJ's sidekick Ponchy drops the needle on the vinyl, three girls jump onto the dance floor. One of them is an *Americana*, her red hair teased and piled high on her head. Her fitted summer dress with spaghetti straps shows off her lean body. Roman sandals flash manicured toenails painted fire engine red.

"*Tramp!*" Carla Thomas sings out to Otis Redding.

"*What you call me?*" Otis sings back.

"*Tramp!*"

"*You didn't!*"

Otis and Carla continue singing to each other while the dancers spread out on the dance floor. The sexy girl with the red nail polish picks up the beat, strutting her body as the crowd cheers. Suddenly, David and Willy shuffle onto the dance floor. The boys move toward her, circling her body, David dancing in front, Willy gyrating behind her.

The crowd gasps when the boys press their bodies against hers. The girl tries to push David away with an uneasy smile.

He moves closer. She looks around but her friends are no longer on the dance floor. My heart races. I can't stop looking at the dancers. Finally, the song ends.

A second of silence is followed by thunderous applause.

"Well, that was some dance," the DJ announces with a nervous grin.

The girl looks a little freaked out. David and Willy are too cool to be bothered.

"Shall we pick a winner?" the DJ teases the crowd.

"Give it to all of them!" someone shouts.

"It was that good, huh?"

The crowd cheers and whistles.

"All right, all right! Copies of the latest release from Stax Records for all the dancers!" The Blue Cloud rumbles with applause. "Ponchy boy, let's dim the lights and get these people dancing!" The DJ's voice is already competing with Arthur Conley screaming "Sweet Soul Music" through the speakers.

Someone taps me on the elbow. It's gotta be David—but it's not. As I walk onto the dance floor, David is heading toward the exit. He turns and looks in my direction. Too bad he didn't see me before walking out the door.

|||

INSIDE THE BLUE Cloud it feels like nighttime, but when the dance ends and we walk outside, the sunlight blinds me. I'm glistening with sweat.

"You look like you took a shower in there," Liz teases.

I ignore her comment, hoping the balmy breeze cools me quickly. Mod dudes and hippie chicks, as sweaty as me, follow us outside. The girl with the red nail polish walks out with her friends. She fans herself with the 45-rpm record she won. Does David like that kind of girl more than me? We start walking away from the building.

"You know that David and Willy are gang members, right?" Liz asks.

"Who told you that?" I snap.

"You're the only two who don't know!" Liz laughs.

"You're making that up," Laura says.

"I'm not!"

"You're just jealous!" Laura hollers.

"Jealous? I didn't see David or Willy ask you to dance."

"They didn't see us," Laura whispers.

"Yeah, right. I hear David is the leader. He and his friends cause trouble and steal stuff."

"What kind of trouble?" Laura asks.

"If they catch a girl alone, they do what they did to that girl on the dance floor."

"They were only dancing, for Christ's sake," I say.

"I hear they do it for real," Liz insists. "You two should know, you went out with them."

Liz pisses me off, but what if she's right? David's and Willy's performance was thrilling. The girl's worried look was not.

"Did they really do *that* to a girl?" I ask.

"That girl dancing asked for it," Laura says. "The way she was dressed and moving her body. Besides, only *cholos* are in gangs. David and Willy are Mods."

Laura makes no sense, but Liz's words make me glad David didn't see me tonight. What will I do the next time I see his beautiful face?

# III

## 48 KATALINA

**I've never seen my mother as a parent.**

Dr. Spock—the doctor, not the alien on TV—taught the world to buy cribs, treat diaper rash, and tend teething. Dr. Benjamin Spock can't help with parenting teens. I find it a mystery how parents, solely responsible for their children's existence, can separate logic and emotion when it comes to disciplining them. Is it even possible?

The August heat and the bus's lack of air-conditioning are affecting my mind. That's the only reason I'd be thinking of Dr. Spock.

"*¡Bajan!*" I scream because the buzzer is busted on this battered vehicle.

The bus screeches to a stop. I hop off and pause under the shade of a tree. Shrubs are rare in this part of Juárez, and the midday sun is beating down on the street.

At my parent's home I find Papá sitting under a makeshift canopy in the courtyard. He's fanning off the heat with his cowboy hat.

"*Buenas tardes, Papá,*" I greet him as I walk through the gate.

He returns my greeting and calls out to my mother, "Febronia! Katalina is here!" Papá turns back to face me. *"Cómo estas?"*

Before I can respond, my mother appears behind the screen door.

"I just fetched a bucket of fresh water. Come in and have a drink." Mamá turns to Papá. "May I bring you a glass of water, *señor?* "

Papá shakes his head.

*"Con permiso."* I excuse myself from Papá and enter the house.

"Have you heard from Ramón? How is he?" Mamá hands me a glass of water.

I quench my thirst before responding. "Ramón doesn't complain." I take another drink. "But I can tell from his letters he's having a hard time."

"I can't imagine life in prison." Mamá shakes her head. "How are you and the children?"

*"Bien.* I feel guilty about not taking the kids to see Amalia and the family as much as I used to but Emilio's treachery makes me ill. And Amalia—I don't know how she can justify her son stealing from family members."

"Someday you'll forgive them. It's difficult to explain such things to children."

I glance through the door at Papá in the courtyard. Lots of things don't make sense to children.

Mamá lowers her head when she catches me looking at my father. "The kids will let you know when they need to visit their relatives."

"The boys don't seem to have a problem with it," I say.

"But I think Inez resents not seeing Amalia. She keeps acting up. She doesn't listen, disagrees with everything...."

The dimples on my mother's cheeks deepen when she smiles. "Sounds to me like Inez inherited your strong will."

I blush, recalling my rebellious years. Life in a small village is different from life in a big city. It terrifies me to know Inez is wandering the streets of El Paso at night. Even now in the middle of the day, she's attending a dance I know little about. I'm ashamed to share my concerns with my mother. What kind of parent loses control of a child?

"*Recuerda*, Inez is a child and children need guidance. Don't abandon her."

"*¡Nunca!*" I cry, as Inez's accusations about leaving her behind in Juárez rise in my head. "Never will I abandon my daughter...."

Mamá and I silently stare at each other. For the first time, I see my mother as a parent.

"My efforts to stop your father when he threw you out of our home only brought turmoil to the family." Mamá wrings her hands. "You were forced to make difficult choices. I hope one day you'll forgive me for being a weak woman. You're doing the right thing by being patient with Inez. *Paciencia* is all we can offer our children."

"*Paciencia*. I'm running out of it and that frightens me."

"You're a strong woman, Katalina. Trust your instincts. No one knows your *niña* better than you. Things may get worse before they improve, but things change."

It's been years since I've felt the comfort of my mother's arms around me. Mamá has tried to heal our wounds but I've dismissed her, afraid that she would not be there when I really need her. Today, when she extends her arms toward me, I hesitate, then fall into them. Mamá's embrace lifts my spirits.

When I look up from her shoulder, Papá is staring at us through the screen door. Will he ever reach out to me? Can I ever forgive him? Forgiveness heals our wounds, but mercy must originate from the heart. I must release the pain and rage that separated us all those years. After all, who am I to judge?

# fall 1967

# ||| 

## 49 INEZ

**First day of school, thrilling and terrifying all at once...**

THE SUMMER OF 1967 is being called "the Summer of Love." The Beatles released a new album called *Sgt. Pepper's Lonely Hearts Club Band*. You can't dance to it, but Mrs. Rogers was right. The Beatles changed music forever with psychedelic rock.

For me, this was the summer Papá went away and missed two big events in my life: entering my eighth year of school and falling in love.

Today is the first day of school, and it's thrilling and terrifying all at once. First graders run around the courtyard like children playing hide and seek, while us eighth graders check each other out: our outfits and hairstyles, and the new kids who transferred.

This year Liz and I are classmates. I already miss Laura.

"Wow!" Liz points across the courtyard. "Look at Mona's hair."

Mona dyed her hair blonde and is letting her Twiggy haircut grow out. Liz waves, Mona ignores her. Mona is busy talking to two new friends, one girl with orange bangs, the other with a serious case of acne that she tries hiding with heavy makeup.

"Who are those freaks with Mona?" I ask.

"How come Mona isn't hanging out with Nicky?" Laura follows.

"I hear Nicky is starting to ignore her," Liz says. "Do you think they had sex?"

"You're such a gossip," Laura scolds.

"She's not the only one with a big mouth," I hiss. Liz wouldn't be such a gossip if Laura didn't help by spilling secrets.

Mona finally walks over with her friends to grace us with her presence. She checks me out. "Hey, I like your Nehru jacket and windowpane stockings."

"Thanks," I say, staring at her friends. They give me the creeps the way they keep looking at me.

"Mona, your hair looks great," Liz gushes.

"Thanks." Mona introduces her friends. "This is Alicia and Irma. They transferred from Vista. So you guys still hanging in the park with David and Willy?" Mona winks at Laura and me. "Did you hear they got busted and were sent away to juvi?"

"What's juvi?" Laura asks.

"Juvenile detention is a jail for kids," Alicia says, running her fingers through her orange bangs.

"Who told you that?" I snap. Was David really sent to prison? What's wrong with boys and men that they're always doing something stupid?

"Who told me what?" Mona says smiling. "That you were hanging out in the park with David and Willy, or that they got caught stealing stuff?"

"Do they send whores to juvi for stealing boyfriends?" Irma asks Mona.

"They should," Mona says. "*Putas* should all be jailed!" Her friends cackle.

These girls are weird, and I'm not in the mood to be hassled.

"I'll see you later." I walk away.

"True bitch!" Alicia hollers.

"What'd I tell you?" Mona says.

The girls' wicked laughter stops me. I turn around and stare angrily.

"Boy, if looks could kill," Irma jokes.

The school bell rings, and everyone scatters to find their new homerooms. Liz catches up to me. I wish she'd stay away. Liz told Mona about our night in the park with David and Willy. What a jerk!

Nicky walks ahead of us. I want to laugh when he enters the room with the number on my registration paper. Does Mona know he's in my class?

"Hi," Nicky says when we meet up at the door. I smile and continue until I find an empty desk. For the first time ever, I sit toward the back of the room. Liz sits across the aisle.

"Hey, Twiggy lover, how was your summer?" Sheldon stands over me, teasing me about my seventh grade project.

I blush. Sheldon grew taller, and his blue eyes never shined so bright. He sits behind me.

A man with a huge briefcase enters the classroom. "Good morning, students. I'm Mr. Hopkins. Welcome to the first day of my eighth grade class." The teacher drops his briefcase on the desk. It lands with a heavy thump. "If you're new to this school, you and I have something in common."

Mr. Hopkins removes his jacket, brushes back a few strands of dark hair peppered with gray and looks at the class. We gasp when he unpacks a stack of papers from his briefcase. Mr. Hopkins smiles.

"Fear not. This is *my* homework, but I'll need your help." He places the papers on his desk. "I'm going to call out names. Please raise your hand if you recognize it as your own and correct me if I mispronounce it. Nothing worse than having your name mangled."

Our new teacher sounds a little whacked. At least he's not a jerk. Things could be worse. Mona and her friends could be in my class.

What a bummer. Mona's back in my life and David went away. Why did summer vacation have to end?

# III

## 50  INEZ

**All the kids snicker at the thought of getting old and wrinkled.**

THE BOTTOM OF Amá Lucia's toes are flat. Is it from walking through all those fields of wild flowers, looking for plants to cook up into lotions and tonics like a mad scientist? Or did her toes go flat walking around her village delivering babies? Abuelita Amalia says that at one time almost every person in San Agustin had been birthed by my great-grandmother.

Last night, Tío Emilio called Mamá to say Amá Lucia was asking to see us.

"*¿Qué paso?*" Mamá asked over the phone. She didn't share Tío Emilio's answer. We just arrived bright and early at their home this morning.

*La viejita* is dying. I can tell because Amá looks tired like Abuelo Sabino before he left us. I don't want Amá to go. Who will read my mind and make weird comments? She's the only one who can curse at the radio while saying her prayers. I pull the sheet over Amá's bare feet while Mamá and Abuelita argue.

"I can't believe you didn't call us earlier," Mamá says.

"I didn't think an invitation was needed for a visit from my grandchildren."

"I was planning to bring them."

"Family has a right to see each other," Tía Patricia butts in.

The women stop arguing and join the circle of restless children surrounding Amá's bed. Eduardo and Carlitos whisper in English while our younger cousins giggle.

"*Por favor,*" Abuelita scolds. "Stop fidgeting!"

"*Déjalos,*" Amá whispers. "Let them jump and scream and be children the way I never allowed you to be."

Abuelita starts weeping.

"*No llores, mi'ja.* Instead of crying, let's pray these children grow as old as me."

All the kids snicker at the thought of getting old and wrinkled. Amá smiles.

"A long life means you have experienced many things, traveled many roads, and met many people. I wish you a long life. *Por favor,* someone hand me my *rosario.*"

Amá's rosary is on the nightstand beside me. I pick up the beads and place them in her hand. Our great-grandmother raises them toward us. Making the sign of the cross in the air, she prays: "*Virgen de Guadalupe,* protect these children, bless them, and guide them." She smiles. "And for God's sake, kids, stay out of trouble."

"Kiss your abuela and go outside," Abuelita instructs the kids.

We take turns kissing Amá Lucia's cheek. My lips touch her thin skin stretched over her hard cheekbone. Amá's hair and breath smell of yerbabuena, clean and fresh as if someone made a rinse of mint leaves. My brothers and cousins scurry outdoors. I stay behind with Abuelita. She throws her arm around my shoulder. I hold on tight to her. If she goes away who will be left behind to hug me?

"Don't be sad, *mi pajarito*, someday we all fly away."

# winter 1967–68

## 51 KATALINA

**Senseless comment spoken in frustration**

THANKSGIVING IS THE first holiday Ramón and I experienced in America. I was housekeeping for a young couple and they asked me to help prepare a traditional Thanksgiving meal. I've never cooked so much food for so few people: biscuits, nut bread, green beans, Brussels sprouts, yams, mashed potatoes, and a huge turkey with walnut stuffing, cranberry sauce, and gravy. Back then, most of the ingredients were strange and unfamiliar. Now I can name all the fixings.

Fisher Slacks distributes free turkeys to employees every year, but I still don't prepare a traditional meal. I'm just thankful to be home with my kids this Thanksgiving Day. It's always more meaningful when we suffer misfortunes.

Doña Lucia passed away soon after our visit. I'll always remember her last words to me.

"Katalina, no one knows a mother's reasoning and I'll never understand Amalia's bias for Emilio but that is how it is. She treated you unfairly. Amalia is my only child. It was impossible not to side with her. I won't be here to welcome Ramón home. Make sure *mi'jo* knows how much I love and miss him. You're a decent woman, Katalina. You understand virtue is the only thing that saves us in our time of hardship. This ordeal has changed your life. Don't let it change your heart. Amalia loves your children. It pains her not to see them."

I promised Doña Lucia the children will visit their *abuelita* often. The day of her funeral, I wrote to Ramón. His response touched me:

"Every night new arrivals cry themselves to sleep at Leavenworth. Cowards, weaklings, afraid of the consequences of their deeds. Last night, after reading your letter about Amá's passing, everyone heard me weeping. Sleep was my only salvation."

I feel for Ramón's loss, but I've had my own calamities to deal with. On Halloween night, Eduardo and Carlitos pulled a prank and stole a hose from a fire truck. No charges were filed. Nonetheless, how humiliating to have the police collect stolen property from our home. Then my friend Lupita swore Inez was downtown when she should've been in school. Inez called Lupita a liar and complained I never believe her.

*Gracias a Dios* for the holidays. Maybe peace will finally reign in our home. I finish writing Ramón a letter and put it aside as Inez enters the kitchen.

"I'm going to Laura's house," she announces.

"It's Thanksgiving Day."

"So what? We don't celebrate Thanksgiving like normal people. You always cook the turkey with rice and beans."

It's difficult to argue with my daughter's candor.

"*Basta*, Inez. Stop being difficult and please wash those zucchini and tomatoes. And you're not going out wearing that skirt. It's so short I can almost see your underwear!"

Inez removes her jacket and throws it on the chair, mumbling.

"*¿Qué dices?*" I demand to know what she's saying.

"It's a miniskirt. It's supposed to be short!"

"Don't get fresh or you'll never leave this house again, *me oyes?*"

"Yes, Mamá, I hear you," Inez mocks.

"I mean it, Inez!"

Youthful, stubborn vanity—Inez has no idea her clothes attract unwanted attention. Women today insist that we shouldn't be judged by our clothing, but we are. Inez stomps off to the living room.

"*¿A donde vas?*" I scream.

"I'm going to watch TV!"

Eduardo and Carlitos volunteered to run some errands, so we're home alone. A man's voice filters from the living room when Inez turns on the TV.

"I have a copy of your book *The Feminine Mystique*, and I'd like to read a quote from it."

The voice of a woman follows. "Please do."

"*Women are victims of a false belief system that requires them to find identity and meaning in their lives through their husbands and children....* You really believe that?"

"Absolutely," the woman replies.

Inez flicks the dial back and forth between the channels.

I holler at Inez: "Stop it! You're going to break the knob. And I asked for your help in the kitchen!"

The phone rings. Inez doesn't rush to answer it. I pick up the receiver.

"*¡Hola, Katalina!*" I recognize my brother's wife, Sarita.

"How are you, are you still seeing Tomás? I hear you two have been spending lots of time together." She's Tomás's cousin.

"I don't know what you mean, Sarita," I say, and pause to hear her reasoning. "Yes, we were spending a lot of time together because of the business."

"His wife says you still meet for lunch, *es cierto?*"

"On occasion. Is there a problem?"

"There's been some talk, that's all."

"Is his wife accusing us of having an affair?" I ask, losing my patience. "Are you? If I am, at least I waited until my husband was in jail, unlike other women in this family!"

Sarita gasps. The woman I'm referring to is no longer in our family. I see Inez standing at the door watching me. A chill runs through my body, and my stomach feels hollow.

"Katalina, as your sister-in-law, I want to make sure all is well." Sarita tries to calm me down. "Besides, I called to invite you and the kids to a New Year's party."

Inez moves to the kitchen counter. She throws the vegetables into a strainer, slams it against the sink and turns on the faucet full blast.

"I'll call you later," I tell Sarita and hang up.

The kitchen counter is splattered with water. I grab a towel to dry it.

"Sarita invited us to their house for New Year's," I tell Inez.

"What a drag," she mumbles.

"*¿Qué dices?*" I want to know what Inez means.

"Why don't you learn English so you can talk with your kids?" Inez whirls around to face me. "Why are you doing this to my father?" Her face flushes, and her eyes tear up. "I wish you were the one in jail!"

Her words pierce my heart. I want to scream but can only whisper.

"I am not doing bad to your father," I say in English.

Inez winces and pushes me away when I reach out for her. "Don't touch me. I'm going out!"

"Don't leave, Inez!" I holler as she stomps out of the kitchen. "If you leave, don't come…" The front door slams before I finish the sentence. What was I about to say: *If you leave, don't come home?*

I must explain that the senseless comment to Sarita was spoken in frustration. Inez needs to know my business with Tomás is over, and so is our friendship.

I rush to the door and dash out to the middle of the road, searching the street for my daughter. Inez is gone.

# III

## 52 INEZ

**Tastes gross but feels wonderful...**

FOUR DAYS AGO we celebrated Carlitos's birthday. Yesterday was Papá's, and today is mine. A few days from now is Christmas. It's a cluster of celebrations at our house. When Papá was home, sometimes he celebrated his birthday with friends and didn't return until morning. Mamá always bought me a birthday cake, even if she didn't feel like celebrating.

This year, Papá's in prison. Mamá hounded me to send him a birthday card. I sent one, but didn't write what I wanted to say. That Mamá and I had a big fight on Thanksgiving Day and I ran out of the house. How I wanted Mamá to stop me, but she didn't.

I roamed the streets, feeling like a stray dog: sniffing, watching, searching, maybe wanting to find a home where people don't leave, die, or cheat. A place without secrets, like the secret I've kept about tattling on my dad to the FBI agents.

How could I tell all that to Papá?

This morning, I'm barely awake when Mamá barges into my bedroom.

"*Feliz cumpleaños, Inez.*" She pats my head and hands me

a letter. "This is from your father. And don't forget, birthday cake tonight."

Mamá stands as if waiting for me to say something. When I don't, she leaves for work. She's been extra nice since our fight. We don't mention her friend Tomás anymore.

The letter from Papá is a birthday greeting: "*Have fun on your 14th birthday, I'll be thinking of you.*" I toss the card aside and pick up the Japanese music box by my bed.

The box was a gift from Papá. He found it when he worked at the Department of Sanitation. I fell in love with the mother-of-pearl inlay on the cover. Inside are Japanese dolls, wood figurines in different shapes and sizes. Why would anyone throw away such beautiful objects?

I took the box and dolls to school when my fourth grade class studied Japan. When our teacher heard us complaining about the heat after lunch, she had us place our heads on our desks. She walked over to the display table, picked up the box, and cranked the lever. The soothing music calmed the class.

I miss all the fun stuff Papá used to bring home from his job at Sanitation. I crank the box lever. Music plays as I get ready for school.

Mona dared us to wear miniskirts because they aren't allowed in school. "They'll send us home to change, and we can hang out," she explained.

"We can hang out at my house," Stevie, one of the other girls offered.

School is such a drag. I'll do anything to stay away, even if it means hanging out with Mona and her creepy friends. I pick out a miniskirt to wear and pack a regular skirt in a bag. This way I can change after we hang out.

I sneak out of the house so my brothers won't see me.

Mona and her friends chuckle when we arrive at school wearing miniskirts.

"We changed our minds," she says and walks away laughing with Alicia and Irma.

Some of the boys in our classroom start howling and whistling when Liz and I walk in.

"Stop it!" Mr. Hopkins hollers and then turns to looks at our skirts. "What are you doing? You know mini-skirts aren't permitted in class. You'll be suspended if this happens again. Go home and change, and return as fast as you can."

Laura and the other girls are already waiting in the courtyard. We rush off to Stevie's house. Once there, she puts music on, and we start dancing. We're in no hurry to get back to class. Then I remember my other skirt. It's in the bag at school.

"Don't worry," Stevie says, "You can borrow one. Come on, let's go change."

The sisters had made minis out of regular skirts and simply let down the hem.

"Hopkins won't notice that we didn't change," Liz says.

Three of us borrow Stevie's skirts. When we return from the bedroom Liz is in the living room holding a bottle of whiskey.

"Hey, look what I found on a shelf," she says. "Let's celebrate Inez's birthday!"

"Put it back," Stevie demands.

"Oh, come on, just a sip," Liz nags.

"My parents will kill me if they find liquor missing."

"They'll never know we touched it."

"How's that possible?" I ask.

"We'll refill the bottle with water," Liz says. "We've done

it before and our mom never noticed. Come on, just a sip to celebrate Inez's birthday."

I don't want to get Stevie in trouble, but I'm curious. "Well, it is my fourteenth birthday."

Stevie finally agrees. Liz pours the liquor into a small glass.

"Drink up, birthday girl," she says, shoving the glass at me.

I sniff and flinch.

"Just gulp it," Laura suggests.

I gulp down the drink and gag when it burns my throat.

"How is it?" Liz asks.

It takes me a second to catch my breath, and another for my body to relax.

"This tastes gross," I say, smiling. "But it's delightful!"

Will anyone notice how happy I am when we return to class?

# III

## 53 RAMÓN

**Shameless disregard of precious people**

LEAVENWORTH PENITENTIARY IS a massive, self-contained institution with canyons of cellblocks reeking of anger, loneliness, and frustration, and the stench of bodies living in tight quarters. Only the cells are small, six-by-nine-feet with cinderblock walls and gray prison bars.

I've only been here six months and already it feels like an eternity. Manual work is the only thing that restores sanity. Good behavior has earned me the privilege to work in the laundry room, time away from my one-room prison.

While waiting for the guard to escort me to work duty, I sit on the cot reading Inez's birthday greeting. It got here weeks after my birthday.

My daughter's birth was the best belated birthday gift I ever received in my life. Like a fool, I often wasted the occasion celebrating with friends instead of family. Holidays were an excuse to escape the rigor of everyday living.

I just experienced my first holiday at Leavenworth. The prison cafeteria served what was supposed to be a Thanksgiving dinner. It turned to mush before you could finish it. The worst part was not having visitors. Number after number was called to join family members in the visiting area.

I sat alone in my cell, emotions swelling: anger, fear, guilt, all due to my shameless disregard of precious people. My reckless nature allowed me to abandon my family, leaving them to face life by whatever means. *¡Inocentes!*

I'll miss Inez's *quinceañera* next year. Katalina and I had started to discuss this special rite in our *niña's* life, that bittersweet moment when a girl enters into womanhood. I wanted to give Inez two parties: one in Juárez, the other in El Paso. Will Katalina hold the event without me, and if so, who will take my place and have the first dance with my daughter?

As I place Inez's birthday card back in the envelope, the inmate across the cellblock hollers, "Hey, baby, are you still celebrating your birthday?"

"Shut up!" The guy gives me the creeps. I say live and let live, but he's been flirting with me since I arrived.

The creep winks, lights a cigarette, and giggles. He lies down on his bed, slides his hand inside his pants, and a few seconds later moans in delight.

"*Maricon,*" I whisper, clenching my fists. "Stay away or I'll kill you."

I've given up cigarettes. Returning in good health to my family is now a priority. It wasn't easy quitting, not when you have to deal with so much filth in here. The guard rescues me from the creep across the cellblock.

"Releasing 84084 for laundry duty!"

Identity is the first thing you lose in the Big Top, your name replaced by a number. Guards also inflict harsh discipline, but nothing compares to the justice imposed by some of the inmates—lost men, void of ethics and humanity.

The guard escorts me and two other inmates down three flights of stairs. The spirit of convicts executed on the grounds here are difficult to ignore when walking through the halls of the Big Top. We step over wet floors being mopped by inmates. Men with nothing to do cheer and jeer at us from their cells.

Once we reach the laundry unit, the guard waits outside. We begin our duties, cleaning and loading the oversized equipment. I enjoy the hard work. It's good exercise, and I no longer get winded since I gave up cigarettes.

The two inmates working with me start discussing Johnny Cash, the country singer who made the news by performing at Folsom Prison.

"Won't buy his music till he comes to play for us folks here at Leavenworth," one of the men says. They cackle at the absurdity of pretending to have the freedom to make such decisions.

I keep to myself during these work sessions, always thinking about the future and my family. When I was sentenced, Ralph Torres said I'll be eligible for parole in three years. With good behavior and a clean record I should be able to go home and finish my sentence on probation. I intend on making things right for my family. I'm so deep in thought, the inmate from the cellblock across the hallway came in without my noticing him.

"Hey, sweetie, look what I found to celebrate your birthday." He grins, pulling a small liquor bottle from a bucket filled with towels.

"Who the hell let you in?" one of the other inmates asks.

"I have friends—and right now, you assholes better leave!"

The two inmates sprint from the room.

"Get the hell out of here!" I scream over the noise of the washing machines.

The creep sets down the bucket and moves toward me. He towers over me. "You're one of the most beautiful men I've ever seen," he says.

"You come near me, and I'll kill you. I'm not into queers."

"I'm no queer, but I'm going to enjoy making you my wife, and you're going to like it!"

The inmate sneers before he lunges at me. I throw a kick. He grabs my foot and pulls me to the ground. He unties his pants, and the grin on his face widens. When he lowers his body over me, I jam my knee in his face. Blood gushes from his nostrils.

"Bastard!" He grabs my collar and lifts me off the ground.

He throws a right cross. Hard knuckles wallop my cheek. We wrestle. I break free and throw another kick; it lands on the creep's groin. My next kick makes him scream, he falls to his knees. I grab a steel bucket filled with soapy water and slam it on the side of his head. He hits the ground.

I start punching. Hard hits meant to hurt someone for hurting others. A beating meant for me. I keep punching until the guards pull me off the creep.

# III

## 54 INEZ

**She holds grudges, it's never over.**

DURING THE HOLIDAYS, people gloss things over with music and cheer. Not this year. We visited Abuelita Amalia on Christmas Day, and she cried whenever anyone mentioned Amá Lucia. And the New Year's party at Tía Sarita's was boring until one of the guests ran outside at the stroke of midnight. He pulled a gun and shot two bullets in the air. Neighbors called the police.

"That's how we welcome the New Year in Mexico!" the man argued when they arrived.

"You're in the United States, sir," one of the policemen said, and issued a warning.

I was glad when the jolly season ended, even if it meant returning to school.

"Welcome back, students," Mr. Hopkins said, "and let us welcome the New Year, 1968!"

That was two weeks ago. Today Mr. Hopkins is still babbling. The only thing I hear loud and clear is the lunch bell ringing. I grab my jacket and leave the room.

Liz catches up with me. In the hallway, we pass Nicky and Sheldon. They're discussing the band Buffalo Springfield.

"The title of the song is *Something Happening Here*," Sheldon is saying.

"No, it's called *For What It's Worth*," Nicky argues.

"So, what *is* happening here?" I ask, adding, "Isn't that song from last year?"

"Good music never grows old," Sheldon says.

Nicky winks at me. It surprises me to see the boys walk off together. Nicky and Sheldon never hung out before. Now it looks as if they've become friends.

As soon as Liz and I reach the crowded courtyard, she runs over and whispers something to Mona. I ignore them and continue toward the cafeteria. Laura is waiting by the entrance. As I approach her someone yanks my hair from behind.

"Bitch!" Mona yells. "I told you to stay away from Nicky!"

She drags me down. I shriek when my body hits the ground. Kids gather around us. I grab Mona's leg, avoiding a kick in the head and pulling her down. We roll, throwing punches in the air, until Mona wrestles her way on top of me and grabs my hair again.

"You think you're so pretty but you look like a monkey!" She bangs my head against the ground. "The only reason boys like you is because you let them touch your tits!"

I finally punch her cheek and keep swinging until I hit her nose. Blood gushes over her mouth and smudges my hand.

"Stop it!" Mr. Hopkins grabs Mona's shoulders and struggles until he finally pulls us apart and yanks us to our feet. Mona's blood splatters on his shirt.

"Fucking whore!" Mona hollers, wiping blood off her mouth. "I'll kill you if you ever look at Nicky again!"

"It's not my fault he doesn't want you, now that he's fucked you!"

The kids watching gasp and giggle.

"Stop it!" Mr. Hopkins warns. "Stop cursing, it only adds to your troubles." Our teacher is out of breath. He lets go of our arms and wipes a stream of blood off his lip with his hand. He straightens his tie and prods us toward the principal's office.

### III

"I THOUGHT YOU and Mona were friends," Principal Brady says, smiling. He sits at his desk. Behind his bald head, bare branches brush against the window.

I'm so pissed, I can't speak.

"What happened?" he asks.

I shrug.

"Come on, Inez. Mona's nose is bleeding, and someone punched Mr. Hopkins in the face and split his lip." His brow creases. "Are you all right? I'm told you took a good bang on the head."

That bitch jumped me! I want to scream, but all I say is: "She beat me up."

"And I want to know why, so I can decide what needs to be done."

I roll my eyes. Why do adults act like they care?

"We've been concerned about you, Inez." Mr. Brady leans back in his chair. "Your grades have dropped, and then there was that incident with the short skirt. Mr. Hopkins informed us that you were acting strange when you returned to class."

I gulp. Teachers are so lame. I'd thought Mr. Hopkins never noticed the alcohol on my breath, although he had kept staring at me with a funny look on his face. Mr. Brady continues.

"We didn't call your mother because it hasn't happened again. I don't know what you've been up to. Perhaps it's time to bring in your mother. What do you think?"

I shrug again. Mamá will kill me if she has to miss work for this.

Mr. Brady picks up his phone and presses a button. When his secretary answers, he speaks into the phone. "Is Mona's nose still bleeding?" He looks at me while listening. "Please send her in."

The last thing I want is Mona by my side, although it's cool to see her hair a mess and a tissue stuffed up her nose. She starts complaining to the principal as soon as she walks in.

"Inez called me a whore!" she says, pointing a finger. "And Liz says she's always flirting with my boyfriend." Mona sounds like a baby.

"You're such a drag. No one wants your boyfriend, and I'm just repeating the name others call you."

"Enough!" Mr. Brady stands up from his desk. "It sounds to me like you have a friend who likes to tell tales. Perhaps you should stop listening to her stories."

I stare out the window behind Brady's head. Mona turns in the opposite direction.

"I think you both learned a hard lesson about friendship today," Mr. Brady says. "How's the nosebleed, Mona?"

I glance over without turning my head, hoping Mona's still bleeding.

"I'm not calling your parents or assigning detention," Mr. Brady says. "But I do want you to shake hands."

No one moves.

"All right, I guess you prefer that I contact your parents."

I don't care if Brady calls the army. Right now I don't have friends, and I'm not shaking hands with a vulgar girl.

After a few seconds, Mona shrugs and extends her hand. I turn away.

"Come on, Inez, be a good sport," Mr. Brady says.

"I didn't start this," I say.

"This has to end, and I want it to stop now."

I slowly raise my hand. Mona grabs it and smiles. It's the same fake smile Mona gave the waitress when she handed over the stolen tip at the drugstore diner.

"Good. Now, Mona, you may return to class but you best heed my warning. I will contact your mother if you continue to misbehave." Mr. Brady turns to me when Mona leaves. "I'm giving you the same warning, Inez. Do you understand?"

"Yes, sir."

"I'll tell you what," Mr. Brady says, returning to his desk. He writes a brief note and hands it to me. "Give this to Mr. Hopkins and take the day off. Go home, rest, and think about what happened today."

Why? I want to ask. Instead I leave without saying a word.

|||

THE KIDS IN class stop talking when I walk in and hand Mr.

Brady's note to Mr. Hopkins. I grab my stuff and leave the room without looking back.

The whisper sounds like a scream in the empty hallway. "Inez!"

I turn and see KiKi, the girl whose mother died, rushing toward me. KiKi's hair bounces with natural curls. Her long limbs remind me of Laura's.

"I heard about the fight. Are you all right?"

"I guess."

"Did they suspend you?" she asks, raising a brow with concern.

KiKi has never spoken to me before. Why is she talking to me now?

"No, Brady gave me the day off."

"Cool."

An awkward silence follows.

"I use to hang out with Mona," KiKi says. "But she can be creepy."

Yes, I know about creepy friends. I feel stupid for trusting mine, and right now I don't trust anyone, especially one of Mona's friends.

"So you and Mona aren't friends anymore?" I ask.

"We're friends, but I don't hang out with her." KiKi's dark eyes twinkle when she smiles. "You know Liz is a gossip, right? She's tells Mona stuff about you to stay on her good side."

"Yeah, okay."

"I hear you punched Mr. Hopkins in the mouth."

"Me?"

"That's what I heard." KiKi grins and makes me smile. "I've been watching you."

"You have? Why?"

"I like the way you dress. And you don't let anyone push you around."

Really, if only KiKi knew. Right now I feel like the biggest pushover in town. What if KiKi is helping Mona to trap me so she and her friends can jump me? I walk away from KiKi. She catches up to me.

"Mona is a bully," she says. "I don't like bullies."

"Yeah, no shit." I turn to look at KiKi's face. Sometimes you can tell when people are lying. "Where did you transfer from?"

"Saint Mary Catholic School."

"Was it fun?"

"Oh, yeah, it was a gas."

We laugh.

"So why aren't you in class?" I ask.

"I have to go to the library. Wanna hang out with me?"

My dress is soiled from rolling on the ground, and my head is starting to feel the pounding. I should go home but decide not to.

"Don't we need a pass?"

KiKi waves a piece of paper. "Got one. I'll add your name."

At the entrance to the library, the librarian checks out my dress.

"I fell."

"Hum…," she grumbles, adjusting her glasses. She looks us over. "I didn't know you were in the same class. Are you studying together?"

"Yes, ma'am," KiKi responds. "We need to study for the spelling bee."

"Spelling books are on the shelves to the right."

"We also need some *National Geographic* magazines," I add.

"Periodicals are in the back." The librarian pauses, then cautions, "Remember, magazines do not leave the library."

We nod, find the books we need, and scurry to the back of the library. Once we're seated, I start flipping through the pages of the *National Geographic* magazine.

"Where is this?" I ask, pointing to the picture of an exotic landscape.

"Another world," KiKi says.

I smile. Hanging out with KiKi helps ease the pain in my heart and my head.

"Be careful with Mona," KiKi warns. "She holds grudges. It's never over."

"Ssssh!" the librarian gestures.

We smile. I can't stop Mona from beating me up again, but maybe KiKi and I can be friends. I hold up the *National Geographic* magazine to show KiKi a picture of a bare-breasted woman standing next to a man. Her breasts remind me of Mona's words. I know one thing. I don't let boys touch me, except David. But is it true I look like a monkey?

I point at the man in the picture.

"The caption says his thingy is wrapped in hemp," I whisper.

We giggle without making a sound.

# III

## 55 INEZ

**"Speak English!"**

MY BROTHERS AND I arrive home from school at the same time. Bummer.

"What happened?" Carlitos asks. "Your dress is dirty, and you have a scratch on your face. Were you in a fight?"

"It wasn't my fault."

"Something brought it on," he says.

"Why doesn't anyone ever believe me?"

"Because you act stupid."

"I'm not stupid!"

"Well, you act it sometimes. Don't you know what people think when you and your friends run around with boys at night?"

The tears I've been holding back gush out and run down my cheeks. Why does Carlitos make everything sound vulgar?

"You're not stupid," Eduardo tells me. "We do dumb things too, but you're going to get in trouble if you don't watch out."

"Are you telling Mamá?" I sob.

"She'll know you were in a fight just by looking at you," Carlitos chuckles.

The boys leave the house while I wash up and change my clothes. Carlitos's words hurt and add to the pounding in my head.

Mona wasn't the first girl to beat me up; I just never told my mother. It happened the first day I attended school in the United States. A girl in my first grade class beat me up for speaking Spanish. "Speak English!" She pulled my hair and slapped my face. I don't remember how I did it, but after that I learned English fast.

I'm sitting at the kitchen table wondering what people are saying about me when Mamá arrives home. Slowly, I turn my head as she walks through the kitchen door.

"¿Qué paso?" she asks as soon as she sees me.

"I fell."

"¿Donde?" Mamá sounds worried. "Where, how, tell me."

"What does it matter?"

"It matters because you could be hurt. Are you in pain?"

"No. Well, a little…"

Mamá drops her bags, moves toward me and places her fingers under my chin.

"You have a scratch on the side of your face. Were you fighting, Inez?"

"Is that all you care about, me embarrassing you by not acting like a *lady*?"

"Stop it, Inez!" She stares at me. "Tell me what happened. Maybe I can help."

"Help me? I don't even know if I can trust you!" I jump up from the chair. "What do you know about friends turning against you?"

Mamá's not a tall woman, but she's never looked so small before. I want my mother to hug me so I can wrap my arms around her and rest my head on her shoulder. She doesn't.

"Why don't you ever hug me like Abuelita? Saving your hugs for someone else?"

Mamá leans back as if I've slapped her face.

# III

## 56 KATALINA

**Mis niños, may you remember my arms cuddling you the day you were born.**

AMOR DE PADRE, my father's love, elusive and unattainable. A touch, caress, embrace was all I needed. What about me was so difficult to love?

What makes parents dismiss their offspring? I've read books listing reasons, but those lists are without reason; I find no rationale in them. I don't want my children seeking these types of answers when they are men and women. Parents never imagine hurting their children. Why can't a child simply be enjoyed and cherished?

*Yerros*; mistakes are inevitable. *Pesadumbre*; regret is preventable because remorse results from actions we have the ability to control. From a child's point of view, I understand the craving for a parent's caress and approval. As an adult, life has marred my vision.

Am I jealous that Inez receives from Amalia the love and attention I longed for as a child? Or am I scarred from my father's indifference? Is this the reason I find it impossible to embrace my daughter and soothe her fears at a most crucial time in her life? Inez seeks something so simple. Why can't I fulfill her need?

When I was blessed with children, I promised to provide a better life for them. Children don't seek material goods until they see them, but love and nurturing are craved instinctively. Seeds are planted in the ground, and we cultivate them until they sprout. Children deserve the same care and treatment.

*Adoro a mis hijos*, my children are my life. *Mis niños*, may you remember my arms cuddling and comforting you the day you were born. Forgive me for failing to assure you with hugs and kisses in your hour of need.

# spring 1968

# III

## 57 INEZ

**"Sometimes myths are just that."**

"'BEWARE THE IDES of March,' the soothsayer warned Julius Caesar, a warning that has forever imbued March fifteenth with a sense of foreboding. What do the words 'imbued' and 'foreboding' mean?" Mr. Hopkins asks, writing the words on the blackboard.

Who cares? I look out the window. This morning, El Paso woke up covered in a brown haze, strong winds stirring the desert sand.

Several students respond to the teacher, and Mr. Hopkins continues.

"Today is March fifteenth, and one must ponder..." He provokes the class by whispering. "Are the Ides of March to blame for this strange weather or is it treason?"

"That sounds spooky, sir."

"Stay on guard, Sheldon, and you'll be fine. But don't turn your back or..."

"Whack!" another student adds, waving his arm like an axe.

"Enjoy your day, students," Mr. Hopkins grins when the

bell rings. "And remember, sometimes myths are just that." He dismisses the class.

I don't wait for Liz after class anymore. Not since my fight with Mona. I questioned Laura about why her sister behaved like a jerk.

"Why didn't you tell me Liz was telling Mona I was flirting with Nicky?"

"I didn't know."

"But she's your sister."

"We don't tell each other *everything*."

I wasn't convinced, but let it go. My new friendship with KiKi made it easier to talk to Liz again, after she apologized. The best part of all is not having to speak to Mona anymore.

The sandstorm is over by the time school ends. Blue skies and bright sunlight greet us when we leave the building. Liz walks behind me. Laura is already waiting for us in the courtyard.

We continue toward the sports field. The girls' track team runs laps in the distance. When we reach the physical education building, Alicia, Mona's creepy friend, stands by the entrance. Her orange bangs almost cover her eyes.

"Hey Liz, you wanna see something?" Alicia calls out. Her body holds open the door to the locker room,.

"What is it?" Liz hollers.

"Come here, I'll show you."

"Should I go?" Liz asks.

"Nah," I say.

"Come on," Alicia insists. "It'll just take a minute."

Liz looks at us, then runs toward Alicia. "I'll be back," she hollers.

We watch Alicia and Liz whispering.

"What does that creep want?" I mutter.

"We'll soon find out," Laura says as Liz runs back to us.

"The track team left all their stuff in the locker room," Liz says.

"So?" I scoff.

"There's money in those purses. Alicia won't tell if we take it."

We turn to look at Alicia. She stands by the door watching us.

"No way. I'm not going."

"Come on, Inez, let's just check it out." Liz dashes toward the entrance before Laura and I can stop her.

Huffing, I follow the sisters down the steps to the basement. Clothing and handbags are scattered on the benches. Liz picks up a pocketbook.

"What are you doing?" Laura exclaims.

We stare as Liz searches through the purse. She holds up a dollar. I remember how easy it was stealing the socks at Sears with Mona.

"Go on, I won't tell," Alicia urges us. "I'll guard the door, but make it fast."

Laura and I rush in, joining Liz, picking up bags and searching through them.

"You better go now," Alicia warns.

She stays inside the locker room, closing the door behind us. We walk away giddy with laughter. As soon as we leave the school grounds, I check out the two dollars I took from two wallets.

The money feels dirty in the palm of my hand. What am I doing? I kind of feel bad, like I felt when Mona took the tip from the waitress in the diner, but it's cool getting free money.

"I don't get it," I say. "Why would Alicia let us take money from the purses?"

"Maybe she's tired of Mona and wants to be our friend?" Laura suggests.

Kiki's warning about Mona suddenly pops into my head. Mona was really pissed off when she heard Liz and I were friends again. Laura may be right, or maybe Mona is using Alicia to get back at us.

KiKi says Mona is a creepy girl.

# III

## 58 INEZ

**Did they put the building by the park because it's a jail for kids?**

MR. HOPKINS CALLS out to Liz and me as soon as we enter the classroom this morning.

"Inez, Liz, please report to the principal's office and take your things with you."

"What did you do now?" Sheldon whispers as I rise from my desk. Liz giggles.

I'm already freaking. My heart races when we reach Mr. Brady's office. He's talking with two men who look like FBI agents. Coach Vasquez and Laura stand with them.

Mr. Brady introduces us to the men.

"This is Inez Ramirez and Liz Vargas."

"I'm Officer Espino, this is Officer Roda," The officer pronounces his Spanish name correctly. He wears a flattop haircut that makes him look like he was in the Army. Officer Espino writes something in a little notebook before continuing. "We're with the El Paso County Juvenile Probation Department. You're being charged with theft on school property."

Liz and Laura start crying.

"Alicia said she wouldn't tell," Liz mumbles.

"Don't blame other people for your decisions!" Coach Vasquez turns away from Liz. She looks like she's going to weep but she's pissed. "I am so disappointed with you," she says staring right at me. "You played volleyball with some of those girls on the track team. You stole from teammates! How could you do that? I'd never have believed it if I hadn't seen you leaving the locker room myself!"

I feel like a creep. I'm also pissed at Alicia. I avoid looking at the coach and bite down on my tongue.

"Coach Vasquez called last night notifying me of the incident," Mr. Brady says. "The school is obligated to notify the authorities when a felony is involved. Now they will notify your parents."

"Theft on school property is a felony," Officer Roda tells us, as if we're supposed to know what that means. "We're transporting you to the Juvenile Detention Center."

Mr. Brady shakes his head at me. He and Coach Vasquez make me feel like I'm the only one who committed a crime here.

### III

EVERYTHING LOOKS DIFFERENT from the backseat of a police car, even an unmarked one. Trees and hills race by as we drive past Memorial Park. I have no idea where the Juvenile Detention Center is located, but after traveling for several miles we head north on East Paisano Drive.

Familiar sights appear. The sign in front of the El Paso County Coliseum announces James Brown's annual appearance. On the other side of the street is Washington Park where my family celebrated Easter Sunday when I was little. We turn right on Boone Street and then left on Delta Drive. The call letters of radio station KELP flash in the distance. I recognize my old neighborhood.

As we drive past the intersection leading to the house we lost on Flower Street, images of Mamá, Papá, and Abuelita appear. What are they going to say when they hear I've been arrested for stealing money? Will Papá and Abuelita still love me once they find out I'm a thief? I close my eyes, not wanting to think.

When I open them up, we're driving by the first school I ever attended, Clardy-Fox Elementary. The school yard reminds me of the day cowboys on horseback chased a bull that escaped from the rodeo held at the Coliseum. Our second grade class stood by the windows while the beast dashed around dodging lassos flying overhead like rings of string. We cheered when we heard the bull was safely returned to the rodeo.

The car's directional starts blinking ten miles down the road. The car pulls into a driveway and stops in front of a low brick building hidden by a row of thick bushes. I don't remember ever seeing this building when my family came to watch movies across the street at Ascarate Drive-In Theatre.

As soon as the officers step out of the vehicle, Liz runs her hand across the screened partition between the front and back seat.

"I feel like a dog back here," she says grinning.

"Shut up!" Laura warns, but we all get a giggle out of it.

I'm the first one out when Officer Espino opens the car door. You can see for miles out here because there are few houses and no tall buildings. Down the road is the entrance to Ascarate Park with its man-made pond surrounded by grass and a few trees. Inside the park is Western Playland. Its rollercoaster and Ferris wheel stand still.

The officers escort us to the entrance of the building. A small plaque identifies it: *El Paso County Juvenile Probation Department, Detention Home Opened 1950.*

Did they put the building by the park because it's a jail for kids?

# III

## 59 INEZ

**"I have no tolerance for troublemakers."**

IT DOESN'T TAKE long for the woman in the front office to check me in. She takes my belongings and says she'll call Mamá as soon as she finishes with Laura and Liz. The woman turns me over to a female guard.

Miss Shea is a quiet woman with red hair and red lipstick. She leads me down a clean, warm corridor without speaking and stops in front of a room with a large window.

The girl in the room screams, "Tell her you want to come in here with me!" She smiles and presses her body against the glass. She's dressed like a boy.

Miss Shea ignores her and unlocks the door across the hall. Once it's open Miss Shea nudges me inside.

"Go on in," she instructs, then warns, "and behave yourself. I have no tolerance for troublemakers." Miss Shea turns to a girl stretched out on the floor. "Put your shoes on. We don't like bare feet here."

The girl looks like an eight-year-old. She wiggles her toes before sitting up between the two cots in the room. The mattresses on the beds are missing. My shoulders flinch when

Miss Shea slams the door behind me and turns the key. The girl and I study each other as the guard's footsteps fade down the hallway.

"I'm Rosa," the girl says, smiling. "What's your name? What are you in for?"

"My name's Inez. We took stuff at school."

"Cool. What'd you steal?"

The bare springs pierce my skin when I try sitting on the bed. I jump up, rubbing the back of my knees.

"They'll bring back the mattresses at bedtime," Rosa says.

She watches me as I stand looking out the wire-mesh glass on the window. The Ferris wheel at Western Playland starts spinning. It's such a soothing ride, unlike the peaks and valleys of the roller coaster that make me scream. Suddenly, the girl across the hall yells out again: "Tell her you want to come in here with me!"

"Shut up!" Rosa screams back.

"Be quiet in there!" Miss Shea bangs on our door.

"Did someone come with you?" Rosa asks. "Sounds like Shea is locking them in."

"Yes, I came with two friends. Why is there a big window in that girl's room?"

"They want to keep an eye on her because she's a dyke. Can't you tell?"

"What's a dyke?" I ask.

"A lesbian. You know, she likes girls instead of boys."

"What do you mean?"

"She likes to do it with girls," Rosa explains.

"You mean, like…have sex with girls?"

"Yep."

I don't know what to say so I look around. "This place is creepy."

"It's creepier out there," Rosa says, leaning her head toward the window.

"How old are you?" I ask.

"I'm eleven. How old are you?"

"Fourteen."

"So what did you steal?"

"Why are you here?"

"My mom's boyfriend tried to rape me."

"What do you mean rape?"

"Don't you know anything?" Rosa says, smiling. "Ma's boyfriend tried to have sex with me. He told her I was lying, so I ran away. The cops found me but Ma doesn't want me in her house. They brought me here until they figure out what to do with me. So what'd you steal?"

It's hard to believe the things Rosa is telling me, but I guess anything is possible when adults who are supposed to be in charge are not. Papá is the smartest man I know, but he's done silly things. Like the time he brought toys from work and I thought they were for me. A few days later I saw them in the yard of a woman who had kids but no husband.

"How can your mother leave you here?" I whisper, sitting down on the floor.

"I guess Ma loves her boyfriend more than me. Now tell me, what'd you steal?"

"Some money."

I spread out on the cold tile floor, slide over on my side, and bite my fingernail until my teeth touch the edge of my thumb. Anything is possible. Mamá left me in Juárez, and she can leave me here. What if she decides she likes that man,

Tomás, after all? What if she does what Rosa's mother did because she likes him more than me? Will I ever go home?

What would Amá say if she was still alive? I remember one time during an overnight visit to Juárez, I started singing a nursery rhyme to my cousins. A group of neighborhood kids looked on. We invited them to play, linking hands in a circle of friendship. No one understood my song because I was singing in English, but more kids joined until the circle spilled out of the courtyard.

Later I heard Amá telling Abuelita, "Inez is a leader, and that's a good thing, but leaders can be lonely because they take risks that frighten people."

I still don't know what that meant, but Amá sounded like she was proud of me. Would my great-grandmother think I'm special now? I don't want Rosa to hear me crying so I try swallowing my tears.

"Hey, don't fall asleep," Rosa warns, "or you'll miss lunch."

I stand up, staring out the window at the Ferris wheel spinning.

# ▌▌▌

## 60 KATALINA

**A situation not worth repeating is
unfolding before me.**

IT TAKES ME a moment to realize that a situation not worth
repeating is unfolding before me: my name blaring through
the speakers, me dashing through aisles of equipment ignoring stares and whispers, and Josie the office manager looking
at me with pity.

"Sit down, honey, and take a deep breath," Josie says.
"Someone's calling about your daughter."

"My daughter?" The indicator light on the telephone
blinks like a warning signal.

"She's not hurt," Josie assures me, then instructs her assistant, "Get a glass of water."

Did Inez miss school without permission? Did she get
into a fight? Is a boy involved?

Josie hands me the receiver. I take a deep breath and push
the button to connect the call.

"Hello?"

"Mrs. Ramirez?"

"Yes, what happened? Is my daughter okay? Where is
she?"

"This is Officer Espino from the Juvenile Probation Department. Your daughter, Inez Ramirez, has been arrested for stealing money from students at school."

My racing heart stops, then starts again, thumping in my head, making my ears ring, muffling the officer's words. I force myself to listen to the details of Inez's arrest.

"She must spend the night at our facility," Officer Espino continues. "Then you have a choice. You may pick up your daughter tomorrow or leave her here. It's up to you."

"Tomorrow, I'll pick up my daughter." Frustration and shame momentarily blur my thinking. "Wait, I must see her tonight!"

"We don't have visiting hours," Officer Espino explains, "and the overnight stay is mandatory. You may pick her up any time after nine a.m."

He ends the call. I hang up.

"Have a drink of water, honey," Josie offers, adding, "Kids do stupid things even when we're watching them. Get permission from your supervisor to go home, Katalina."

Shame renders me speechless. I nod and leave the room. If people gawked when I left Fisher Slacks in the middle of the day, I don't remember.

# III

## 61 AMALIA

### No lessons learned from strangers

LIKE RAIN FALLING from dark clouds, I predicted this day when my son Ramón moved the children to *el otro lado*.

"*¿Qué has hecho, Katalina?*" I screech. "What have you done to my *niña*? I warned you about taking Inez away!"

Katalina's shoulders slump. It's easy intimidating women abandoned by family. Their self-confidence suffers with them. She paces, hasn't sat down since she arrived with news of Inez.

"Help me! I must bring Inez home."

Katalina's in pain. She lights her third cigarette. Pleads and worries. Behavior caused by the realization of her failure as a parent. For years, ever since Katalina took Inez away, I've waited for this moment. *Virgin Purísima*, thank you for answering my prayers! Katalina's heart is breaking but *mi niña* is the only one who matters now. This time I won't let her go.

"*Claro.*" I pause to light a cigarette. "Of course we must bring *la niña* home. This is where she belongs, not with people who have no interest in her well-being. No lessons learned from strangers."

Katalina ruined Ramón's life. *Gracias a Dios*, she has

enough sense to ask for help before making the same mistake with Inez.

We will bring Inez home, restore her honor. No one has to know about this shameful incident. When Inez is old enough, she can marry a respected man.

*Mi niña*, I will help you.

*¡Qué deshonra!* The disgrace of having to protect children from parents.

It happens.

# III

## 62 KATALINA

**Is it possible Inez's behavior is not my fault?**

WHEN ONE CHILD breaks your heart, all your children suffer. Carlitos and Eduardo prepare their own breakfast while I drag myself out of bed. Remorse drains my body; Amalia's accusations ring in my head. Groggy from lack of sleep, I walk into the bathroom, lean over the sink and brush my teeth. A deep breath eases the pain inside me but nothing can erase Carlitos' and Eduardo's revelations.

Yesterday, the boys found me in the kitchen where I sat staring at the wall. When I told them what happened, they just glanced at each other. As if they'd known all along.

"*¿Qué?*" I demanded, alarmed by their lack of surprise.

"Inez has been getting into a lot of trouble," Carlitos said.

"She got into a fight at school," Eduardo added. "And people are saying things about her and boys...."

I didn't want to hear it but they told me about Inez meeting boys at night.

"People are so quick to judge," I retorted. "Inez is just a child."

"She can get pregnant." Carlitos's statement startled and

shocked me even when Eduardo made it clear they weren't sure the rumors were true. What an awkward conversation to have with children.

This morning anxiety flares up as my thoughts keep spinning. *Como dos gotas de agua*, like two drops of water. *Tal para cual*, the apple doesn't fall far from the tree. Simple sayings say a lot, if we listen. I'd probably add my own proverbs if my daughter wasn't the one being described.

Inez not only broke the law, she violated a code of ethics. Criminal behavior is unacceptable regardless of gender. Such conduct stains a woman's virtue. *Orgullo*; pride complicates reason but dignity defines humanity.

After breakfast, Eduardo and I travel to the El Paso County Juvenile Detention Center. Officer Espino greets us and offers to assist me when we meet with the director of the facility. "*Yo hablo Español*," he says.

"*Gracias*," I say, grateful to spare Eduardo this unpleasant task. "I speak some English."

"I will translate as needed."

My son waits in the lobby while the officer and I meet with the director of the center.

"Mrs. Ramirez, this is Director Henken."

The director exhales smoke and quickly stubs out the cigarette in an ashtray. He stands up from his chair and offers his large hand for a handshake.

"Please sit down, Mrs. Ramirez. I understand Officer Espino explained the reason Inez was arrested." The director taps a pencil on his desk. His blue eyes twinkle when he speaks.

"*¡Qué vergüenza!*" I declare.

"Shameful," Officer Espino clumsily translates.

After a brief pause the director picks up the conversation.

"Females express love, anger, and fear with the same passion. These emotions test our limits when expressed inappropriately. Your husband is incarcerated, correct?"

"Yes, sir."

"Was Inez close to her father?"

I think back on all the times Ramón was teased about Inez being his *consentida*. I love all my children, he would reply. But everybody knew, Inez was the apple of his eye.

"Yes…. They were—are close."

"Children don't process loss like adults. They internalize it and feel responsible for it. In the case of a parent getting into trouble, children often grow angry when they can't help. A father's absence is always difficult on a girl. Under these circumstances it could be tragic. If Inez was aware of her father's love, she felt abandoned when he left. Girls often replace a parent's love with promiscuous behavior, drugs, or alcohol. Others reject love to protect themselves."

Everything the director said makes sense except one word. I turn to Officer Espino and ask him to translate the word promiscuous.

"*¡Imposible!*" I exclaim. "Inez is only fourteen. How could a child be promiscuous?" I stop, recalling Eduardo and Carlitos's warning. Even if the rumor about Inez meeting boys at night is false, it's troubling.

My body trembles. Attempting to ease my pain, I wonder: Is it possible Inez's behavior is not my fault? A deep sigh clears the webs in my head. Of course it's my fault. Ramón and I are both to blame, he for going away, me for not paying attention.

"We are still researching children's behavior," the director continues. "In the meantime, we lock them up. I see troubled kids from ten to sixteen years of age. All are on the brink of becoming juvenile delinquents. It's my job to stop them from becoming hardened criminals. Your daughter isn't a criminal. She doesn't belong in this facility filled with complex systems and procedures. Inez needs guidance and stability."

"This is why I'm here to take my daughter home."

Ramón and I wanted the best for our family. We expected challenges in America but did not prepare ourselves for this new world. If we had, perhaps we would've been stronger, more able to face events that tested our ethics and values.

I want to ask the director if it's possible to stop children from repeating their parents' mistakes. I keep the question to myself.

# III

## 63 INEZ

**I'd give anything for Mamá's scrambled eggs with pinto beans and warm tortillas.**

SIX O'CLOCK IN the morning: that's the time Miss Shea wakes us up and marches us into the dining room. It's the first time I get to see Liz and Laura, their sleepy eyes filled with fear.

Miss Shea stands guard over eight drowsy girls sitting at a table, staring at bowls of cold oatmeal. I'd give anything for Mamá's scrambled eggs with pinto beans and warm *tortillas*. I almost spit out the spoonful of oatmeal.

Talking is not allowed at the table. The only sound comes from silverware striking dishes. The air feels moist as if someone is boiling lots of water. There is no odor. The only aroma in the room comes from recently awakened bodies.

We have fifteen minutes to eat. When we finish, some girls stay behind to clean the dining room and kitchen. The rest of us march back to our rooms. The mattresses have been removed. I curl up on the floor, flashing on the image of Liz and Laura. Looks like I'm not the only one frightened in here.

It felt creepy last night, sleeping in a strange room, on a strange bed, next to a stranger. Rosa talked late into the night while I watched the lights of Western Playland. I could almost hear people screaming on the roller coaster ride. How weird, not being able to walk out the door and go to the amusement park I've enjoyed for years.

Time stands still in here. I don't know how long we've been back in our cells before I hear Miss Shea opening a door in the hallway.

"Hey, someone's getting out," Rosa says. She jumps up from the floor and runs toward the door. "It looks like your friends." She stretches her neck to look out the small window.

I join Rosa at the door, shove her aside and stare into the hallway. Liz stands waiting while Miss Shea releases Laura from her cell. The sisters walk away without looking back.

I lie down on the floor again and stare at the ceiling. My heart races. If Mamá leaves me in here, do they have a school I can go to? What if I meet a girl like Mona and we have to share a room? Only two of my fingernails haven't been bitten to the quick. I bite one of them off.

Rosa jumps up when we hear Miss Shea opening our door.

"Let's go," the guard says, pointing at me. "Your mother's here to take you home."

"Take me with you," Rosa hollers as I leave.

# III

## 64 KATALINA

**Qué tormento; loving someone who resents you is torture.**

MI CORAZÓN PALPITA; loud thumps beat against my chest, then my heart breaks at the sight of Inez's wrinkled dress, disheveled hair, and bloodshot eyes. Was my daughter allowed to sleep, was she fed? Inez looks frightened—until she sees me. Suddenly, her shoulders roll back, and she takes on an air of defiance.

"Sit down, Inez," the director says. He watches as she hesitates before sitting next to me. "We want to know if you're ready to go home."

"Of course I want to go home."

"We know you *want* to go home. The question is: are you *ready* to go home."

Inez avoids eye contact. She sits perfectly straight, perfectly still.

"Your mother wants you home. You should be grateful and apologize for your behavior."

Inez gazes at the floor, then glowers at me. *Qué tormento;* loving someone who resents you is torture.

"It's not uncommon for children and parents to be at odds

with each other. Unfortunately, Inez, you broke the law." The director picks up a manila folder from a stack on his desk. I see Inez's name on the label. Director Henken drops it on his desk and continues. "Next time there will be serious consequences, and your mother will have no say in the matter. Do you understand?"

Inez nods before lowering her head. She shoves away my hand when I reach out to her. *Palpotear*: to handle carelessly— is this what I've done to my daughter?

"Let's get you home, Inez."

I thank the director. It's crucial to reach the door before I break down crying.

# III

## 65 INEZ

**They should all apologize to me!**

THE STREETS OF El Paso aren't as lively as the avenues of Juárez. El Paso doesn't have street vendors pushing carts or carrying trays filled with fruit and candy. In Juárez, the rhythm of *cumbia* music blares from storefront speakers and drifts through car windows. The music seems to make everyone smile on the bus Mamá and I are riding.

It doesn't brighten up my day because we're on our way to see Abuelita. How mad will my grandmother be? Will I still be her *pajarito?* A bump in the road causes Mamá to slam against me. I lean toward the window to avoid touching her.

"Are you all right?" she asks.

I nod.

It's been three days since Mamá brought me home. We haven't spoken much. Even Carlitos has been quiet. My brothers and Mamá look away when I catch them watching me. It feels like they're afraid to do or say things around me. Mamá said something about making sure I get help from somewhere. Help for what?

Mamá spoke to Principal Brady on Friday. He agreed to

let me return to school with a month of after-school deten-tion. I wish I didn't have to go back on Monday. What are the kids in my class going to say? Will Lalo call me names? And what about Sheldon, will he still tease and flirt with me, now that I've been in jail?

I don't care!

I don't know if I want to hang out with Liz and Laura any-more. The only person I want to be friends with is KiKi, even though she's still friends with Mona. Mamá once explained that if your friends are friendly with people you don't like, just stay away when they're together. Maybe that'll work because Mona and I will never, ever be friends again.

Mamá's face, reflected on the bus window, looks sad. It was wrong to steal, and maybe I should've apologized to my mother. Is this why she's bringing me to Juárez, to leave me here because I didn't say I was sorry? But everyone misbe-haved, not just me. Papá did something stupid, that's why he's in jail. Mona is a jerk, her friend Alicia is a rat, and the sis-ters—maybe they were never really my friends.

They should all apologize to *me*!

# ||| 

## 66  KATALINA

**I wanted my baby with me.**

MY ELBOW NUDGES Inez when a passenger calls out our stop. She follows me off the vehicle and lags behind as we make our way to Amalia's house on the hilltop. The Ramirez family is sitting at the kitchen table when we arrive.

Amalia jumps up and runs to Inez. "*¡Mi vida!* What have they done to you?"

The tender moment between my daughter and her grandmother causes a surge of rage and sadness in my heart.

Amalia releases my daughter and looks her over. "This is where you belong." She addresses Inez but turns and glowers at me. "Nothing but trouble since you left this house."

"Again?" My voice must have betrayed my emotions because everyone stares at me. Are they afraid I'll make a scene?

"*Cálmate, Katalina,*" Emilio says.

I want to scream that I'm tired of having the same conversation about whose home is best for Inez. I run my fingers through my hair. "*Por favor,* don't tell me to calm down." My jaw tightens as I speak.

Emilio gets up from the table, picks up a pack of cigarettes, and walks outdoors. Inez sits at the table next to her cousins. The kids gawk at her.

Patricia pushes away from the kitchen table and stands. She turns to her children. "*Váyanse!*"

Once they leave the room, my sister-in-law moves toward me. "What Amalia's trying to say is that your children would've received more attention if all of you had stayed with the family."

I turn to Amalia. "I thought we agreed to put our differences aside for Inez."

Patricia and Amalia look at each other.

"*Tal vez,*" Patricia says. "Inez can stay with us awhile."

"*¡No, señora, jamás!*" My heart stops: What if my daughter wants to stay? I can't blame her for wanting to get away from the person who failed her as a parent.

"*¡Eres egoísta!*" Amalia screams at me.

"You were going to leave Inez with strangers so you could work!" Patricia says.

"I wanted my baby with me."

"How many times must you tell yourself that?" Amalia taunts me.

"*¡Maldicho!*" I cry out. "Malicious words!"

"I'll say it again: Inez would not be in this mess if she had stayed here!" Amalia insists.

"*¡Basta!*" Inez screams.

# III

## 67 INEZ

### Home

**NO ONE IS** more surprised by my outburst than me. Where did I get the nerve to shush my mother and grandmother? Maybe I'm just tired of them fighting. Now that I have everyone's attention, I don't know what to say. I stand facing the women in front of me.

"Am I coming home with you?" I finally ask Mamá.

"Stay with us, *mi pajarito*," Abuelita interrupts. "I'll cook all your favorite meals, and we can visit *el ranchito* any time we wish. Remember how much fun you had visiting San Agustin with your cousins?" Her voice trembles, but she doesn't weep.

I loved living in Mexico with my grandmother but now I want to live in America with my family. Mamá wants me with her. Otherwise I'd still be in jail. And she just told Tía Patricia I'd never stay here again. I'll behave and teach Mamá more English so we can do things together, like go to the movies. When Papá returns, we can go to the movies as a family. I turn to my mother waiting for her answer.

"I..." Mamá looks at the floor "Stay here if you want."

My throat clenches as I rush into my grandmother's arms. I hate America, and I never, ever, want to leave Abuelita!

"*Mi pajarito.*" Abuelita nuzzles her face in my hair.

Without moving, I gaze at Mamá. That's when I see it. Tears welling up in her eyes, telling me what I need to know. My mother always wanted me with her. Mamá needs me.

"*Te adoro,*" I whisper to Abuelita and draw back to look at her. Abuelita's smile disappears. I gulp, swallowing my tears. "I love you, and I'll always be your *pajarito*. I'll come visit."

My grandmother draws me close. Her body gently quivers; a silent sob brushes my ear.

"My little bird is flying so far away; *tan lejos.*"

I release my grandmother. No one speaks. I look around at a familiar room that feels so different, then reach for Mamá's hand. She flinches but my fingers weave our two hands into one.

"Let's go home." I release her hand and start to move away. She pulls me back. Mama looks at me as if wanting to say something. I hug her; gently her arms wrap around me.

# Acknowledgments

As with any production, these ventures are never accomplished alone. Thank you to Jean Huets at Circling Rivers for making this happen; to authors Gerald and Lorry Hausman for your expertise and guidance; to friends who took time to help me along the way; and to the staff of Pine Island Library, in Bokeelia, Florida, for keeping the printer going. And especially, *MIL GRACIAS para mis familias Rangel, Mascorro, Alcantar, y Lira:* your pride and spirit continue to guide me through life.